Kalpana's Dream

Kalpana's Dream

JUDITH CLARKE

FRONT STREET
Asheville, North Carolina

Originally published in 2004 by Allen and Unwin

Printed in the United States
Designed by Helen Robinson
First U.S. edition

Library of Congress Cataloging-in-Publication Data:
Clarke, Judith, 1943-
Kalpana's dream / Judith Clarke.—1st U.S. ed.
p. cm.
Summary: While an English class of 7B students at
Wentworth High in Australia struggle with a six-week essay
assignment answering, "Who am I?," one child's great-grandmother
arrives unexpectedly from India to follow her dream.
ISBN 1-932425-22-5 (alk. paper)
[1. Great-grandmothers--Fiction. 2. High schools—Fiction.
3. Schools—Fiction. 4. Australia—Fiction.] I. Title.
PZ7.C55365Kal 2005
[Fic]—dc22
2004021005

Doctor Ignatius Grace's biblical compliments
to his wife and daughter come from
"Song of Solomon," King James Version of the Bible.

FRONT STREET
A Division of Boyds Mills Press, Inc.
A Highlights Company

*For Erica and Susan
and Nirmolini—with thanks
and to Rashmi Desai
for help with the Hindi*

 Contents

Little Again

"Know what? We're little again!" gasped Kate.

Neema couldn't get a breath to answer. She was too hot, and her mouth was dry from the kind of panic she'd last felt on her first day at primary school, when through the window she'd watched her mum walk down the path, through the gate and out into the street, leaving her behind. She didn't feel herself at all.

Which was what Kate had meant, of course. Last year, just six weeks ago in December, Kate and Neema had been the big girls of Short Street Primary. Now, on their first day at Wentworth High, they were little again, right at the bottom of the school.

They felt like crying; they couldn't even find the room for their next lesson, which was English with Ms. Dallimore.

"Where *is* it?" wailed Neema. "Where on earth's Block A?"

"I don't know," Kate answered dully. The photocopied

map they'd been given that morning at assembly seemed too crowded and difficult to understand.

So they were lost as well as little. Wentworth High was huge: a crazy jumble of unfamiliar buildings, courtyards and playgrounds, steep steps up and down the hillsides, echoing covered ways. They'd been running since the first bell at lunchtime, like puzzled rats caught in a maze. At any moment the second bell would go, and there was no one to ask for directions. The playgrounds, noisy and crowded only a few minutes back, were now silent and deserted; everyone had vanished, swallowed down into the school.

They stumbled at last into a small paved courtyard. On one side was a low gray building Neema thought she might have seen this morning on the Year Seven tour.

"I think that's the library."

"I *know*," Kate snapped, exasperated, wild eyes almost popping from her head. "But where's *Block A*?"

"Lost?"

They spun around. As if by magic, three kids had appeared on the steps of the library: two girls, one fair and one dark, like Snow White and Rose Red, and a tall, thin boy, too gangly for a prince, with a battered old skateboard tucked beneath his arm.

Neema felt an odd little flicker of recognition when she saw the boy. Surely she knew him from somewhere? But her head felt so thick and heavy, and her ears were buzzing from all that running round, and when she glanced at the boy again—no, of course she didn't know him, she'd never seen him before. Sheep, shepherd, new lamb—the words darted unexpectedly across her mind, as if the sight of the boy had brought them there. Why? He didn't look the least bit sheeplike.

"Where do you want to go?" he asked them, and now she thought there was something familiar in the kindness of his voice, and the way the skin round his eyes crinkled when he smiled …

"Room 27, Block A," she heard Kate saying. "English with Ms. Dallimore."

"Ms. Dallimore!" Rose Red rolled her eyes, and Snow White murmured, "Oh dear!"

"The Bride of Dracula!" said Rose Red.

"The Bride of Dracula?" echoed Neema faintly.

"Is she that little pointy one?" asked Kate, alarmed. "In the—"

"In the hat?" finished Neema. They'd both noticed this teacher at assembly, a stringy little woman, all edges and sharp angles, wearing a stiff orange dress that resembled a coverall, and a funny floppy red velvet hat. Beneath the hat a pair of vivid black eyes had glowered round at everyone. What subject did *she* teach? Whatever it was, Neema and Kate had prayed she wouldn't be teaching them.

"Oh, no!" Rose Red giggled. "That's Mrs. Drayner— Draino, we call her. She's the chief school cleaner."

"She always comes to assemblies."

"She says she wants to see the kind of individuals who can turn a school into a pig sty."

"Ms. Dallimore's the one with the dark red hair."

"In the long swirly skirt—"

"The pale one—"

"*Very* pale."

"And getting paler." Snow White and Rose Red exchanged knowing glances. The boy with the skateboard looked away, and as he did Neema thought there was something familiar in the shape of his fine, narrow nose.

"Ms. Dallimore *looks* all right," said Rose Red, suddenly reassuring, as if she might have said too much.

"No harm in her, you'd think," agreed Snow White. "Except for those essays of hers, of course."

"Now they *are* tricky."

"How?" asked Kate uneasily. She hated English; it was her worst subject. She was simply no good with words; her brain seemed to set in concrete when she had to write down her thoughts. "How are they tricky?"

"Mmmm." Thoughtfully, Snow White twirled a lock of her long blond hair. "Well, it's like, they look easy, but when you start, you find they're really hard."

"I reckon He chooses the topics, you know?" Rose Red whispered to Snow White.

"Could be," agreed Snow White.

He? Who was He? Neema and Kate felt more lost than ever, as if, besides the maze of buildings, classrooms, new subjects, and new teachers, there was an extra hidden world at Wentworth High which they'd have to get to know. It was all too much. "Oh," sighed Kate wearily.

"Don't worry," said Snow White kindly. "She won't give you an essay for ages, seeing as you're new."

"And she mightn't be here for long, anyway," added Rose Red mysteriously.

Why? Neema wondered. Why wouldn't she be? There wasn't time to ask; the second bell rang out.

"Oops! Gotta go!" Snow White and Rose Red rushed up the steps to the library.

"But where's—"

"Block A?" said the boy. "Come on, I'll show you." He led them to a small flight of steps at the corner of the courtyard. Shepherded them, thought Neema, though it wasn't a word she'd normally have used.

"Down there, see?" He smiled at them again, that smile Neema felt she knew. "That building at the bottom is Block A, and Room 27 is the first one on your left, in through the big glass doors."

"Did you see how short those girls' skirts were?" exclaimed Kate as they clattered down the steps. "They were *heaps* above the knees. I *told* Mum, but she wouldn't listen to me. *I'm* going to take mine up the minute I get home."

Neema didn't reply. If she'd been listening to Kate properly she would have said there was no way she was taking up her skirt. She liked it long; it covered her big knobbly knees. But Neema wasn't listening. She was still thinking about the boy with the skateboard, wondering how a person could seem so strangely familiar when surely you'd never seen him in your life before.

—

Inside the library, Snow White and Rose Red settled themselves at a small table near the window. Their real names were Sarah Dunne and Ivy Stevenson, they were in Year Eight, and they'd both had Ms. Dallimore for English only the year before.

"Poor kids," observed Sarah thoughtfully as she arranged her folders on the table.

Ivy was frowning. She'd just found an old sandwich in the bottom of her school bag, left over from last term. "Yuk! What poor kids?"

"Those two little girls in the courtyard. Did you see how long their skirts were? Year Sevens, eh? Remember when we were new?"

"Oh, don't remind me!"

"Hey, look!" Sarah pointed to the window. Out in the courtyard a tall red-haired lady in a long swirly skirt was hurrying toward the steps that led down to Block A.

"She's late again."

"Mmm. Perhaps she's been out to lunch with her boyfriend. With Him."

Ivy studied the teacher, frowning. "Do you think it's true, what people say?" she asked Sarah. "That her boyfriend really is Count Dracula?"

Sarah shrugged. "Could be."

"No one's ever seen him, though—only that big black car that picks her up from school. It could be anyone behind those tinted windows. Might be her mother, even."

Sarah grinned, craning her neck for a last glimpse of Ms.

Dallimore. "She's definitely getting paler, though—and in the summertime!"

Ivy nodded. "Oh, very definitely."

At another table in the library the boy with the skateboard sat thinking about the slender dark-haired girl he'd met in the courtyard a few minutes back, the girl who'd sent a strange little shiver of recognition tingling down his spine. The boy's name was Gull Oliver, and though he was in Year Eight he was new to Wentworth High.

His skateboard sat beside him, propped against his bag. "Who was she, mate?" he asked it softly. "Who?"

Someone he'd known a long time ago, thought Gull, so that now she looked entirely different: that was the sort of thing that was always happening to him these days.

There was a fairy story he'd read when he was little, about some guy who'd fallen into an enchanted sleep beneath a mountainside for years and years and years—and when he woke up, no one knew him, and everything was changed. It was a little like that with him. He hadn't been asleep, of course; it was simply that when he was halfway through Grade One at Short Street Primary, Dad's job had taken the whole family away to Germany for seven years. It was the strangest thing, how people you'd last seen as little kids were now almost grown up, how faces had lengthened and hair grown darker and voices deepened; and yet there was always something familiar about them, so that after a few minutes you realized who they were. With the dark-haired girl it was the eyes: he'd seen those eyes before, a deep clear brown with tiny flecks of gold, fringed by dark sooty lashes and fine arched brows. Yet he couldn't remember who she was, and he knew from that funny little tingle that had fluttered down his spine that she must have been someone special to him, back when he was six years old. And if she was special, why couldn't he remember?

Gull frowned. The way he couldn't remember was a little like losing something. When you mislaid some small object you didn't much care about, you always found it quickly; but when one of your treasures went missing, you could search and search all over and it was nowhere to be found. "We'll find her, mate," he whispered to the skateboard. "We'll find out who she is, you'll see."

Kalpana's Dream

It was one o'clock on a brilliant summer's afternoon when Neema and Kate walked down the corridor of Block A toward their first class with Ms. Dallimore. But far away in a little country town in India, where Neema's great-grandmother lived, it was still early in the morning.

Her name was Kalpana, and she'd been up for hours.

She always rose early. Old people didn't need much sleep: there were too many memories, nipping and twitching, tugging you awake. And dreams: two nights ago Kalpana had been young again; she'd felt the gentle touch of her mother's hands at her waist, folding the pleats of the marriage sari; she'd seen her mother's face, with tears standing in her eyes. "Please, Ma," she'd whispered, "please don't cry."

"Tears of happiness," her mother had replied.

Kalpana saw many faces in her dreams, but never the one she wished most of all to see: the face of her young husband, who'd died when he was barely twenty. No, not once had she seen her Raj's face, and even its memory was fading.

She crossed to the window and stood there. Everything outside seemed smaller today: the cobbled courtyard, the tamarind tree, even the big iron gates that screened the house from the road. Smaller, and lonely too—abandoned, as if she had already gone away.

Because last night Kalpana had made up her mind. She would do it, she would go; she would fly to Australia to see her great-granddaughter, Nirmolini. It was a whole nine years since she'd seen her last, and the child would be twelve now, almost grown.

She would travel by herself, she had decided on that. When you were old, you had to do new things. Her family would fuss, of course: her nephews and grandnephews, her daughter Usha most of all. They would want to come with her, carrying her suitcase and shawl, dogging her footsteps, telling her what to do. Let them fuss! She was going on her own!

"Ah!"

Kalpana turned. Her old friend Sumati stood in the doorway, barefoot, a giant pail of washing hanging from one arm. There were washermen in plenty in their little town, but Sumati distrusted them all. "Thieves and liars, every one!" She preferred to do her washing in her big old laundry pails, exactly as her mother and grandmother had done theirs, in their small, rock-strewn village way up in the hills.

When they were children, Sumati had been Kalpana's little

nurse, and when they were grown up she'd become Usha's nurse. Now that she and Kalpana were old, Sumati was more like a big sister—a rather bossy one.

Sumati took one look at Kalpana and set the pail down with a clang. "So you have decided."

"Yes."

Sumati clapped her hands. "I knew. The moment I saw your face, I knew. And you will go on your own?"

Kalpana nodded.

A wicked grin lit Sumati's leathery old face. "Ah!" she crowed, waving one hand in an easterly direction, toward the new part of town where Kalpana's nephews and grand-nephews lived in their big modern houses that Kalpana found ugly and cold. "There will be much squealing over there," Sumati said gleefully.

"Let them squeal," replied Kalpana. "What else can they do? They can't lock me up, can they?" She grinned back at her friend. "We are in modern times."

"Exactly so," replied Sumati, "modern times." Then she added slyly, "Your daughter will not like it either."

Kalpana shook her head. "Poor Usha."

"She will come hurrying from Delhi to bother and fuss and boss. Ah, these teachers! Always boss, boss, boss."

"How would you know?" asked Kalpana, smiling. "You never went to school."

"Thanks be to heaven! But the village school was near to my father's house. I passed it daily—such things went on there in that place! Small boys hardly taller than this"—Sumati gestured at the laundry pail—"slapped about the ears for talking, or getting answers wrong. What foolishness was that? Everyone knows a slap will make the thoughts fly from your head. Of course, your Usha would not slap; she was always a kindly child." She sucked her teeth and frowned. "But bossy, still."

"Bossy," Kalpana agreed. She paused and then added, "You're sure you don't want to come with me, Sumati?"

"Ah, no. That is your journey; I have my own. I will go to my sister Lakshmi's place in the hills. She has been begging me to make a visit for a long, long time." Sumati picked up the bucket and went out into the hall. Then she stopped and called back, a little shyly, "You will come back, though? You won't stay there?"

"Of course I'll come back. This is my home, and yours."

When Sumati had gone, Kalpana went to the window again. The blue sky dazzled, vast and empty, except for a big dark bird circling high above the trees. Her little great-granddaughter had loved the Indian sky.

"I have had that dream again," Kalpana whispered to the great black bird. The dream she'd been having all through this winter, over and over again. The dream of flying—not in a plane above the world, as she would do very soon, on her way to Australia; no, not like that at all. In the dream Kalpana flew by herself, like magic, her feet skimming only a little way, a hand's height, over the ground. Small pink clouds sailed above her; on her right there was water, a blue lake reflecting sky, and on her left, a bank of silvery, unfamiliar trees. It was no place Kalpana had ever seen, yet she knew with utter certainty that it was a place that existed on the earth—a place that she would one day see. In the dream she flew faster and faster, the cool breeze fanning her cheeks, her sari floating out behind. And she knew that if she flew fast enough, a small crack in the world would open and she would see Raj's face again. She would see that special smile he kept for her alone, the one that brought the tender light into his eyes and made the hidden dimple show, that secret little hollow at the corner of his mouth.

Kalpana turned away from the window. The great bird circled once more, slowly, and then flew away, across the river toward the great desert, over the ragged rooftops of the dusty little town.

.
.
.
.
.
.

Count Dracula's Essay

It was three whole weeks before Ms. Dallimore handed out her first essay to 7B.

WHO AM I? she printed in big, bold letters on the board.

Easy. It didn't look as if He had chosen it.

Because by now most of 7B knew who "He" was. They'd heard the rumors the Year Eight kids passed around: how Ms. Dallimore's boyfriend—the driver of the big black car that waited for her every afternoon outside the gate—was Count Dracula. "She's getting paler," the Year Eight kids kept whispering. "Paler and paler, every day."

They said Count Dracula chose the essay topics for Ms. Dallimore. But "Who Am I?" didn't seem the sort of topic a vampire would select. All the same, a chorus of complaint rose from the ranks of 7B.

"But, Miss! That's baby stuff."

"Dead boring!"

"Embarrassing!"

"We've done it heaps of times."

"All though primary school."

"You start off in Prep, with this drawing, and your name—"

"Next year it's in printing."

"And then joined up."

"Longer and longer—"

"More and more words—"

"I want you to forget all that," said Ms. Dallimore. "All those other times. This time I want you to *think*—" and she turned round and wrote the word up in the same big, bold letters, so firm and fast you could see the chalk dust spurt into the air. "I want you to use your brains and your imaginations!" She smiled radiantly around the classroom. "Writing can be like flying when you do that," she said.

Flying??? There was a disbelieving silence from 7B, so thick you could hear the chief school cleaner and her Hoover noisily entering the staff room at the bottom of the hall. "Disgusting!" snorted Mrs. Drayner. "What a rats' nest! A hole! Worse than the kiddies, any day!" The rest of her grim displeasure was drowned in the outraged roar of her machine.

Kerry Moss spoke up. Her voice was a low, ragged growl. "My mum says it's unhealthy to think," she told Ms. Dallimore.

"Then you can ask her to see me," the teacher answered calmly.

There was a gasp from the other kids who'd gone to Short

Street with Kerry: Kate and Neema, Big Molly Matthews, and Blocky Stevenson. Tough Mrs. Moss had been the terror of the Short Street teaching staff. That day in Grade Four, when she'd bawled out poor Mr. Pepperel, Mr. Pepperel had—left. He'd packed his bags and gone; he was teaching in the country now. "Somewhere along the Lachlan," Neema's doctor dad had told her, for Mr. Pepperel's old mother was one of his patients. "Somewhere along the Lachlan," her dad had caroled, "at a place called Booligal. Sounds like it should be set to music, doesn't it? Poor Mr. Pepperel!"

Frail Ms. Dallimore would be no match for Mrs. Moss, thought Neema.

Or would she? Neema didn't believe the Dracula story—how could you?—but there was something a little unearthly about their English teacher. She was so very pale and her curls were such a dark vivid red, as if her blood was rising up into her hair. Could she be sick? Was that why she was so pale? But Ms. Dallimore didn't seem sick: her movements were brisk and energetic, and when she spoke about writing, and *thinking*, her big eyes glowed, and her pale face took on a kind of shimmer, like the luster of a pearl.

"Think," Ms. Dallimore went on serenely. "Think at strange times."

Strange times???

"When you wake suddenly in the middle of the night, and everyone's asleep except you—don't you feel like a different person then? A secret person? And mightn't that secret person be the real you, that rare person who's never been on earth before? Mightn't you then, in the quiet, hear the heavenly music of your own soul?"

Huh?

It was all too much for Blocky Stevenson. His hand shot up. "Miss!" he called sternly. "Miss!"

"Yes?"

"Miss, I'm not *rare*. I'm just an ordinary kid who likes football. Aussie Rules. But"—Blocky folded his arms across his solid chest—"I'm not a leatherbrain."

"Leatherbrain?" echoed Ms. Dallimore.

Big Molly Matthews creaked round in her chair. "It's what Mr. Crombie—he has us for history—calls boys who love football, Miss. Boys who play football even in the summer!"

"I didn't say 'love,' I said 'like,' " muttered Blocky.

"Mr. Crombie thinks they've got shriveled brains," Molly went on. "Shriveled brains like leather, see? He says for every goal they kick they lose a hundred brain cells, and in the summer, it's a thousand—but that's not true, is it, Miss? Because if Blocky had no brains, then he wouldn't care about being called a leatherbrain, would he?"

"I suppose not," replied Ms. Dallimore, a little uncertainly.

"And Miss, what you love shows who you are, doesn't it? So if you wrote about something you love, you'd be writing about your real true self, wouldn't you?"

"Oh, *yes!*" replied Ms. Dallimore.

Molly beamed at her. "So I'm going to write about my baby shoes!"

A muffled groan rose from the Short Street kids. Molly Matthews' baby shoes! She'd talked about them at Show and Tell for years: how beautiful they were, how soft and tiny, how she could remember her mother's hands fastening the two little buttons on the side ...

Molly glared round at them. "I'm going to!" she cried. "I can, can't I, Miss?"

"Yes, of course you can, Molly."

"*See*?" Molly flounced in her chair triumphantly, and the chair gave a mighty creak.

Molly Matthews was a big, big girl. Her hands were big, and her feet, and her kind face was round as a plate—a very big plate, a Christmas plate you could fit a whole turkey on. There were kids from Short Street who said Molly Matthews had never worn those shoes. They were made of soft blue leather, tiny as fairy slippers. Even when she was five, both little shoes had fitted neatly into one of Molly's broad pink palms.

"It stands to reason," Kate had said to Neema when they were both only in Grade Three. "She'd have been an enormous baby, with enormous feet. Her gran might have bought those shoes for her, like she says, but I bet her mum could never squash them on."

It was one of the few things Kate and Neema disagreed about, because Neema felt certain that there would have been a time, even if it was a very short time, a few days, or perhaps a single week, when Molly's new pink feet would have fitted perfectly into those fairy shoes.

Neema's gaze drifted toward the window: across the playground she could see three boys helping Mr. Lazenby carry sports equipment, and one of them was the boy she'd met outside the library on her very first day at Wentworth, the one who'd seemed so strangely familiar. His back was toward her, yet she knew it was him—something about the set of his shoulders and the way he moved. And once again those words came drifting oddly into her mind: sheep, shepherd, lamb …

"Ms. Dallimore?" Brainy Jessaline O'Harris raised an earnest hand.

"Yes, Jessaline?"

"Ms. Dallimore, when does the essay have to be handed in?"

"Oh, six weeks or thereabouts," said Ms. Dallimore casually.

Jessaline gaped at her, and so did the rest of 7B. Six weeks? It was ages; in six weeks a whole long summer vacation could pass, a kitten grow into a cat, a baby learn to smile. You could grow your hair long, fall in love and out again, get slim, grow fat, learn Russian, become an entirely different person. Jessaline twitched at her long, skinny braids. "Ms. Dallimore?"

"Yes, Jessaline?"

"Ms. Dallimore, why have we got so long?"

7B listened, and Ms. Dallimore's radiant smile shone over them again. "So you can think," she answered, "and imagine, and—and learn to fly!"

Sweet Lucy

Kate raced along Lawrence Road in the direction of Kindly Kidcare, her bag banging on her shoulders, dodging old ladies out shopping with their carts, and stragglers from the primary school who chanted at her, "Kate thinks she's great! Just because she goes to high school!"

She was late. Her little sister Lucy would be waiting, giving poor Miss Lilibet what Mum called Lucy Hell. She was late because she'd hung out at the gates with Neema and the other kids from 7B, complaining about Ms. Dallimore and her essay and the mysterious fact that she'd given them six whole weeks to do it, which meant she must be expecting something truly special ...

And as they'd stood there, grousing heartily, who should come by but Ms. Dallimore herself—long skirt swirling, her dark red hair fizzing with some kind of weird electricity. "Thoughts flying already, I see," she called as she swept past them, heading for that waiting big black car.

Not even Tony Prospero, whose dad ran Lawrence Motors, could identify the make of the glistening black car. It was huge and solid, with a long sloping bonnet and big spoked silver wheels. "Like a bloody hearse," growled Kerry Moss. Its windows were black too, tinted darkly against the light—you couldn't hope to get the tiniest glimpse inside. Ms. Dallimore wouldn't be at Wentworth High much longer, the Year Eights kept hinting darkly. Soon, perhaps very soon, Count Dracula in his big black car would speed her away to his castle in Transylvania.

Which was a fairy tale, of course, thought Kate. All the same, when Ms. Dallimore started in about thinking and imagination and *flying*, and heavenly music of the soul—when she started giving out wacky homework—you couldn't help hoping the fairy tale might be true.

Because what did Kate have to write about? She was ordinary, like Blocky Stevenson. There was nothing the least bit unusual about her, and her family was ordinary too. She didn't have exotic parents like Neema had: a glamorous Indian mother who worked at the university, and a doctor dad who, when he was a baby, had been found in a cardboard box on the back step of a children's home …

"Oh!" Kate skidded to a halt. Across the busy road, she saw a small square girl in a paint-smeared smock, all by herself, gazing entranced into the window of the hardware store. Lucy. Lucy where she shouldn't be, again.

"Lucy!" Kate fought her way grimly through the heavy

afternoon traffic, the streams of trucks and fuming buses, the angry hooting cars. "Lucy, what are you doing here?"

Her little sister turned. Ignoring Kate's question, she pointed to the window, where a big shiny mulching machine was displayed behind the glass. "Katie, if you put a person in there, a bony old person like Lilipet, and switched it on, would—"

"You're not supposed to *be* here. You know you're supposed to wait at the nursery school for me."

"You were late. All the others had gone home. There was only Lilipet there."

"That doesn't matter; you still have to wait."

"I was helping you," said Lucy, as she often did.

"What?" Kate was breathless and angry from her struggle across the road. She'd almost been run over by a pale pink florist's van. Looking down at her little sister's bland face, she felt a sudden painful jab in the middle of her chest and thought it might be actual hate. If only Count Dracula would spirit *Lucy* away.

"I saved you walking all that way," said Lucy virtuously, "like—like *her*." She pointed down the road, and Kate turned to see a small, disheveled figure hurrying anxiously toward them: Miss Lilibet.

Poor Miss Lilibet was breathless too, her face all flushed and blotchy, big black hairpins tinkling to the pavement at her feet. "Oh, Lucy dear, I'm so glad you're safe and sound!" She put out a hand to pat Lucy's arm, but Lucy flinched away. "So careless of me!" Miss Lilibet exclaimed. "What will your mother think?"

Nothing, thought Kate. There was no way she was telling Mum that Lucy had run off again.

Miss Lilibet pushed back a straggle of wispy hair. "I turned my back for just the merest second, and she was gone. Vanished into thin air. She's so, so—" Miss Lilibet stared at Lucy, who stared sternly back. "So quick."

"Yes, she is quick," agreed Kate.

"And so determined."

"Yes."

Now they both considered Lucy, their gaze fixed on her small square chin and the way it jutted, firmly, from beneath her rosebud mouth. Lucy would be a match for any vampire, thought Kate.

"There's never been another child got out before," Miss Lilibet went on fretfully. "Never once!"

"You can go now," Lucy told her, waving a small dismissive hand. "My sister's here."

And Miss Lilibet obeyed! She obeyed a four-year-old! Kate watched the small, sad figure plodding down the road, shoulders drooping, head lowered in defeat. That was one thing she'd never be when she grew up, decided Kate: a nursery school teacher, no way!

"You shouldn't run away from the poor thing," she scolded Lucy.

There was no reply. Stealthy as a thief, Lucy had scuttled off again. Kate spotted her almost at once, down at the bus stop, talking to—oh no! Kate's heart gave a little jump inside her chest—a group of Year Twelve girls from Wentworth High, resplendent in their brilliant scarlet sweatshirts! And—and Lucy was dancing round them, one small arm stretched out, one chubby, square-nailed finger pointing at their knees. "It's snowing down south!" she was chanting gleefully. "Snowing! Snowing!"

It was a saying of their gran's to which Lucy had taken a fancy, ever since she'd heard Gran murmur the words to another old lady in the supermarket. The old lady had looked down at the white edge of slip showing beneath her hem, tugged at a hidden strap, and whispered, "Thank you, dear."

"Snowing down south!!"

The Year Twelve girls never wore slips beneath their tiny skirts. They didn't know what Lucy meant. Neither did Lucy, really.

"Down south?"

"In Tasmania, darling?"

"No! No! Down there!" Lucy pointed at their knees again.

"Isn't she cute?"

"Darling."

"Sweet."

Lucy did look sweet, Kate would grant them that. She was very small, and everything about her was square: her short, sturdy body, her face, the glossy chocolate-colored hair that was cut straight all around so that only the tips of her ears showed beneath it, like drops of rich pure cream. Yet whenever some stranger in the street said "sweet," Kate fumed inside. Oh, it was all right for them! They didn't have to live with her, they didn't have to share a room!

"Why is she here on her own, though?" wondered a thin, spiky-looking girl with a prefect's badge pinned proudly to her chest.

"What's your name, sweetie?"

"That's for me to know and you to find out," replied Lucy, in the manner of her gran.

"Are you lost, darling?"

"No!" Lucy stamped her little foot.

The girls laughed. "Ooh, she's cross with us!"

"Look at her eyes! They've gone black—like raisins."

"No, they haven't! My eyes are beautiful! My gran says! Yours aren't, though—yours are like, like—"

Kate rushed up. "Lucy, come on now, we've got to get home."

The Year Twelve girls gazed at her with disapproval.

"Are you her sister?" demanded the spiky prefect.

"Yes," mumbled Kate.

"How come you left her on her own? She could have gotten lost."

"Or run over."

"Anything."

Kate flushed. "I didn't leave her on her own. She—she got away from me." Kate heard her voice sounding lame and flustered, a little like Miss Lilibet's.

"You should take proper care of her," said the spiky one repressively.

"She's only small, you know."

"And sweet."

"Snooty Year Twelve snobs," raged Kate as she marched Lucy off along the street. She bet none of them had little sisters. Or if they did, you could bet they didn't have to share a room with them, or do their homework with a Lucy hanging round their neck. Or listen to her snoring when at last she'd gone to sleep—really big snores, the kind you might expect from a construction worker who'd had a heavy day on site.

How on earth was she going to get Ms. Dallimore's essay done, when everyone agreed that instead of being easy, it might turn out to be really hard? How was she going to concentrate, to think, to imagine, to—to fly? With Lucy there?

If only Dad would finish her room, the little room he was making for her by enclosing half of the back verandah. It was nearly finished: all he needed to do now was put the windows in, the windows that would look out over their big yard. Then she'd have peace, and a private place, and a latch on the door to keep Lucy out. "Ready by Christmas," he'd promised her last year. And then, "Ready by the time school starts." Now it was "Ready by Easter," and Easter was weeks away. And Kate just knew that when Easter came closer and she started asking him again, Dad would say, "Ready by winter"—or else start giving his favorite answer, which was "Soon."

Their house was full of "soons": taps that dripped and drawers that stuck and roller blinds that wouldn't roll ...

"Kate! Katie!" Lucy was tugging at her arm.

"What?"

"You're not listening! You didn't hear what I said!"

Kate sighed. "What did you say, then?"

Lucy beamed at her. "I'm going to have Ovaltine when I get home—and not in milk! Out of the tin, with a big, big spoon!"

"No, you're not. Mum says it's bad for your teeth."

"I am," said Lucy. "Am! Am! Am! And you'd better not try and stop me or I'll—"

"You'll what?"

With her free hand Lucy reached into her pocket and took out something truly horrible: it looked like a crow's whole wing. She brandished it at Kate. "Or I'll knock you down with a feather!" she said in Gran's voice again.

Kate's lips twitched; she simply couldn't keep from smiling. As Mum said, Lucy was hell, but you had to laugh at her sometimes.

.
.
.
.
.

Nirmolini

Two weeks passed. No one in 7B had got very far with Ms. Dallimore's essay, not even Molly Matthews, who normally couldn't wait to write about her baby shoes. Jessaline O'Harris was the only one who'd really started, and starting it was as far as Jessaline had got. "It looked so easy," she'd told Kate and Neema earnestly one study period in the library, "but do you know, I simply couldn't get a grip on it." Brainy Jessaline had shaken her skinny braids in bewilderment. "And that's not like me at all." She'd fished a crumpled piece of paper from her pocket and shown it to them. "Look!"

Kate and Neema saw a single messy paragraph, with more crossings-out than words. Jessaline had scrunched it into a ball and tossed it on the library floor. "I can't believe I did that," she'd said, shaking her braids again. "I normally don't litter."

"Who Am I?" was turning out to be so tricky you could almost believe it *had* been thought up by Count Dracula.

Neema had a room all to herself, the kind of peaceful private place that Kate longed for—and she had no little sister to hang about her neck—but like Jessaline O'Harris, she was having difficulty. Because when you started thinking about who you were, really were, it *was* somehow hard to get a grip. Neema only had to think about that first day at Wentworth High, when she and Kate had felt little again, and then back to Grade Six at Short Street, where they'd felt quite grown up: which one was real? And if neither was really you, then what was?

"Think at strange times," Ms. Dallimore had told them. "When you wake in the middle of the night …"

But these past few weeks, when Neema woke, all she thought of was the boy with the skateboard, who'd brought that odd little picture of sheep and shepherds tumbling into her mind. Sheep and shepherds, little new lambs . . Why? Why did the boy make her think of that? She'd wake up and lie there in the dark, puzzling it over, trying to find a clue.

And she never could. She'd seen him again only this afternoon, skating so fast down Lawrence Road he looked like a flying boy. That was a good name for him, decided Neema: the flying boy. He hadn't noticed her. Why should he? Why did *she* notice *him*?

Neema looked down at the almost empty page. She'd been sitting at her desk for ages, and all she'd done was write the title and her name, and the name was sort of wrong. Her real one, the name Mum and Dad had given her when she was born, was Nirmolini.

—

"Nermo, Nermi—what?" Miss Lilibet had floundered, on Neema's first day at nursery school.

"Nirmolini."

"What a mouthful! We'll call you Lena, eh?"

"But I'm *Nirmolini!*"

"Sounds like an ointment!" shouted a stocky little boy in a football jersey, a shock of rough black hair standing in spikes from his wedge-shaped head. His own name was Brian Stevenson, but later on at the place Miss Lilibet called Big School, the kids would start calling him Blocky. "Nermolene!" he'd gone on shouting. "That icky, gooey stuff you put on when you've got a rash!"

"Don't be rude, Brian," Miss Lilibet had chided. "And it's Germolene, not Nermolene." She'd turned back to Neema. "But you see what I mean, dear. Nirmolini's too difficult, too hard for people to get their tongues around, especially little people. And you might get teased when you go to Big School. You wouldn't like that, now would you?"

Neema had shaken her head.

"Right then." Miss Lilibet clapped her hands. "Hands up who likes 'Lena'!"

Everyone had put their hands up, except for Blocky, who muttered, "I like Nermolene."

Priya, Neema's mum, hadn't liked the new name either. "Lena! Ugh! It's horrid. What's wrong with your proper name?"

"Miss Lilibet says it's too hard. For little tongues."

"Hard!" scoffed Priya.

"She says I might get teased. At Big School."

"Ah!" sighed Priya. "Oh, well. But not 'Lena,' 'Neema.'"

So Neema she'd become, and everyone had forgotten "Nirmolini," except for Mum and Dad. Dad had chosen the name himself, an Indian name, even though Dad was just an ordinary Australian. "It means 'beyond price,'" he'd told her, and then he'd gone on dreamily, "Beyond rubies, beyond pearls ..."

Her dad often talked this way, like poetry or the Bible. He knew a lot of stuff from the Bible, because of Sister Josephine and the other nuns at the Children's Home. It was Sister Josephine who'd given him his own name, Ignatius, after the saint on whose birthday he'd been left at their back door. "Lucky it wasn't Valencia," Dad liked to joke, because the box he'd come in had once held oranges, and "Valencia, Premium Quality" was printed on the sides.

The nuns had also given him his second name: Grace. Because it was by God's grace they'd found him that night, Sister Josephine believed, before the heavy rain began; by God's grace she'd opened the kitchen door at midnight, to bring her gumboots inside. "Ignatius," surely, was even more difficult for little people to get their tongues around, yet Dad had never been teased at school and he was proud of his difficult name. "Ignatius Grace MD" was inscribed proudly on the shiny brass plaque outside his office.

"Nirmolini," Neema whispered, trying her real name out loud. It didn't sound so peculiar now, as it had, quite suddenly, on that first day at Miss Lilibet's nursery school. Though it didn't sound like *her*, it suggested another girl altogether—someone older and more serious, a graceful girl who didn't have knobbly knees. Neema pushed the sheet of paper to the back of her desk and went down to her dad.

"Dad?"

"Yup?"

"Dad, what would you answer if I asked you, 'Who am I?'"

His head bobbed up from the book. "That's easy." He grinned at her. "You're my precious daughter, my enchanting Nirmolini, who"—he pondered for a moment, and then went on—"who looks out like the dawn, beautiful as the moon, bright as the sun, majestic as the starry heavens …"

Which was lovely, but obviously, for Ms. Dallimore's essay, simply wouldn't do.

Neema walked down the hall to her mum's study. She paused outside it, hearing the soft flutter of the computer from inside. She opened the door a crack and peered into the room. Her mum sat gazing at a row of symbols flickering on the screen: she was a math professor and she was in love with math. She'd fallen in love in her first year at college in Delhi, where she'd had a very tiny, very old teacher named Miss Dabke. Mum often dreamed of little Miss Dabke. She dreamed that the old teacher stood by her bedside and whispered, "Heavenly! Ah, heavenly, Priya! The mathematical music of the spheres!" Watching the tender, rapt expression on her mother's face—it really was the expression of someone listening to heavenly music—Neema felt it was a pity to disturb her. Softly, she closed the door.

As she passed the living room, her father called out, "Shulamite maiden, come back, that we may gaze upon you!"

Shulamite maiden! It sounded so beautiful, like that older, graceful girl her real name conjured up in Neema's mind.

"Hey, Nirmolini! Neema!" Dad called in his ordinary voice. "Neem! Come and hear this joke old Mr. Flannery told me in the office today! He said it was a special one, for you! And after you've heard it, let's be devils and have a long, long game of Monopoly!"

A very small battle went on in Neema's breast, between Ms. Dallimore's essay and Dad's devils: the devils won easily. She'd start her essay another day; handing it in was weeks and weeks away.

In a house on the other side of the park, Gull Oliver lay staring at the ceiling of his room. His skateboard sat propped against the bedside table, very close to him. "'Night, mate," he said to it, and then switched out the light.

He couldn't get to sleep, though; he kept thinking of Nirmolini. Because it *was* her, that Year Seven girl he'd seen outside the library with Katie Sullivan on the first day of term, the girl with the gold-flecked eyes who'd sent that shiver of recognition tingling down his spine. When he first knew her, seven years ago, those eyes had often been red and swollen with tears.

Well, who didn't cry on their very first day at primary

school, or *feel* like crying? Funny how he'd met her on her first day at Short Street, and then at Wentworth on another first day. Sort of—magical. He'd spent ages trying to remember who she was because who could have imagined that funny little weepy red-faced kid would have turned into this slender, graceful, dark-haired girl? He could have asked her name at school, but somehow he'd wanted to find out in some other, more special way. A more enchanted way, he thought: either to remember by himself, or to hear the name spoken, out of the air, like luck or fate.

And it had come: two weeks ago on the playground he'd heard someone call out to her, "Neema!" and then he'd known for sure. Neema had been the name everyone had called her, even back at Short Street; only Gull had known her real name was Nirmolini. Mrs. Flannery had told him. Mrs. Flannery had been headmistress at Short Street in that year before he and his family had gone to live in Germany; she was the one who'd begun the "shepherd" program for the little kids starting school.

"Now, Gull," she'd said to him on the day before the new children arrived, "your new lamb is called"—she glanced down at her file—"Nirmolini. Isn't that a beautiful name? Nirmolini Grace."

It was beautiful, Gull thought. It sounded like a tiny little song, all by itself. It was the most perfect name in the world.

"Nirmolini," he whispered softly to the skateboard. "Her name's Nirmolini, mate."

.
.
.
.
.
•

$\mathcal{B}$oss! $\mathcal{B}$oss! $\mathcal{B}$oss!

Half a world away, Neema's great-grandmother Kalpana had begun her packing. There wasn't much of it: seven white saris, underwear, a spare pair of sandals, a single soft, embroidered shawl

Kalpana's daughter Usha stood watching; she'd rushed down from Delhi the minute she heard the news.

"You're not taking *those*?" Usha's gaze fixed on a shabby old bedroll and battered water-carrier leaning against the wall.

"Of course not," replied Kalpana, calmly folding the shawl.

"They are for my own journey," said Sumati. "To my sister's place. Do you think your mother would take such things on a plane?"

Usha looked embarrassed; indeed she'd thought just that.

"Do you think we are feeble-minded and know nothing

of the world? Do you think we do not know there is water on planes, and little blankets, light as air? Perhaps you think she is taking her chickens along, and the neighbor's goat also?"

"No, of course not," said Usha, flushing. "But—"

"Always 'buts' with you," cried Sumati. "Buts and fuss and boss!"

There *were* "buts," though, reflected Usha. Lots of them. A ticket and passport, for a start, not to mention the visa. Mention it she did.

"You'll need a visitor's visa," she told her mother, "and that can take a very long time." Perhaps the long wait would put her mother off the whole idea …

"Passport, ticket, visa—everything is done!" crowed Sumati, pointing to a shiny folder on the bureau. "See?"

Usha picked up the folder and leafed through its contents. Sumati was right; everything was done, even the visa stamped firmly into the brand-new passport. Usha was astonished. How had two old country ladies managed all of this?

"We have been to Ahmedabad!" said Sumati proudly. "We have been to Bharat Travel, and also visited your father's friend."

"My father's friend?"

"Kanti Shah," said Sumati.

"You would not remember him," said Kalpana, a little sadly. "You were only a baby when last he was here."

"Kanti Shah has a son who works in the embassy," explained Sumati, "very high up." She snapped her fingers.

"Two weeks and it was done. He is quick, that one."

"Even as a child he was quick," said Kalpana, smiling.

Sumati chuckled at the memory. "*Bapre*! See his mother run!"

Usha studied the ticket. There was a three-hour wait in Hong Kong. Her mother would have to change planes! For her age, she was very fit and healthy, but she'd never traveled out of the country or even flown on a plane, and the only language she spoke was Hindi. Terrible visions began to rise in Usha's mind. Was it possible, these days, to actually get onto the wrong plane? To fly somewhere else, without knowing you were doing so? She pictured her mother arriving in Moscow, believing it was Sydney, waiting at the arrival gate with her shabby little suitcase, wondering why Priya and her family hadn't come to meet her. Or Reykjavik, thought Usha wildly. Or Addis Ababa!

"Why go on your own, Ma?" she said. "You could have come with me when I visited Priya last summer."

"I had not decided then."

"You could come with me next year."

"I want to go now."

"I'll come with you, then! I—I can take time off from school!"

Kalpana shook her head.

"Well, what about your nephews? Your brothers' sons? I'm sure one of them could go with you—"

"Those!" The word burst from Sumati's lips. "What would your mother want with them? Boss! boss! boss! All the time—worse even than you! Your mother would put one little foot out, to take a step, and they would shout, 'Not there! That is wrong! Here, here, Kalpana, put your foot here! Here is proper place!' "

Kalpana smiled. "Exactly so."

"But, Ma, you need someone with you!"

"I want to go on my own," repeated Kalpana, narrowing her eyes and drawing her soft old lips into a thin, determined line.

Her daughter had seen that expression on her mother's face only once before—long ago, when Usha had won the scholarship to Delhi University and her uncles had said they would not allow her to go. A young girl in a big city, all alone! What would become of her? And who would marry such a girl, a girl who'd been to university, who'd been living on her own?

But her mother had been determined. "Why waste the gift of cleverness?" she'd asked the uncles. "Why turn your back on what is given?" She'd set her lips and narrowed her eyes at them, and one by one the uncles had given in.

Usha changed tack. "Does Priya know you're coming?"

"We wrote to her last week," said Sumati.

Last week! Usha glanced at the date on the ticket, scarcely ten days away. "They won't get it in time! Letters take three weeks, sometimes even four! I'll have to phone! I'll have to phone right away!"

Sumati clapped her hands. "Shoosh!" she ordered. "Shoosh now! Stop this fussing, forget this phoning, and be off with you to bed. Tomorrow will do for that; we have no phone anyway."

"But—"

"To bed at once. You look very bad, Usha. All wrinkled and worn out, older than my own mother even, when she was ninety years. This is what fussing will do for you!" She clapped her hands again. "Off you go, now!"

Usha went. Why was it, she asked herself, that whenever she came back here, she felt small as a child again? She didn't go to bed, though; she drew the line at that. Why should she do what Sumati said? She was a grown woman, not a four-year-old. She was a grandmother, a teacher, headmistress of St. Ursula's Ladies College! She would go to the post office and ring her daughter's family from there.

Clutching her handbag, Usha crept down the passage and out through the back door. She crossed the courtyard and reached the big iron gates beside the road. There she stopped. The gates were old and squeaky; to open them would bring sharp-eared Sumati running from the house to scold her all over again. There was a gap in the hedge farther down; Usha knew it from her girlhood when she'd crept out at night to stand like a lovesick fool outside Hardev Bhari's house. Hardev Bhari! Usha tossed her head. What an idiot she'd been! Worse than her own Year Tens, who were giving such trouble at St. Ursula's, throwing notes to the boys of St. Leo's, turning their hair green, attempting to dye it in fashionable Western colors.

Usha found the gap, though it seemed somewhat smaller

than she remembered. Overgrown, thought Usha as she struggled through. Or was it she who was overgrown? "Must go on a diet," she muttered as she set off toward the town.

The students at St. Ursula's Ladies College, even the green-haired ones, would have been surprised to see their distinguished headmistress hobbling down that dusty country road. Her smart Delhi suit was badly rumpled, the blouse hanging out of the skirt. On her feet she wore Sumati's cracked old leather sandals, because in her hurry Usha hadn't been able to remember where she'd put her shoes.

She hadn't remembered the time either. The post office was shut; it was ten o'clock at night. No light shone in the windows of the postmaster's house, but Usha battered grimly on the door. She'd hobbled all this way in the dark, her feet were killing her, the soles of Sumati's sandals seemed to be fastened on with nails. She was making that call to Priya! Priya's family had to know! Usha checked her watch again and did a rapid calculation. Ten o'clock here, so in Sydney it would be afternoon, it would be about half past four.

"Who was that?" the postman's wife asked as he stumbled back to bed.

"The one from Delhi. Kalpana's child."

"The schoolteacher?"

"That's the one." He pulled the cotton quilt up to his chin. "Always in a hurry, always rush, rush, rush."

"Who was that?" asked Ignatius as Priya came back from

answering the phone. It was half past three in the morning, the very middle of the night. Back in India, Usha had counted the time difference backwards instead of forwards. "It's not Mrs. Oliver's baby coming early, is it?"

"No," said Priya.

"Or Mr. Crombie's kidneystone?"

Priya shook her head.

"Or—" he grinned at her, "old Mrs. Pepperel's indigestion?"

"None of those," answered Priya.

"Then who?"

"Mum." Priya's eyes were round with amazement. "Guess what? Nani's coming! Nani's coming here!"

·
·
·
•
•

Nani's Coming

Neema's dad burst out with the news at breakfast. "We've got a surprise for you!"

Neema looked up from her bacon and eggs. "A surprise?"

"A really big one!" Her dad's face was glowing; he nudged at her mother's arm. "Go on, Priya. You tell her, it's your family, after all."

"Nani's coming," said Neema's mum.

Neema gave a small, startled jump in her chair. "*Gran?*"

Oh, no! Not Gran again. Gran was so *bossy*! She couldn't stop being a headmistress for a single minute, not even when she was on vacation. Every moment she was at it: asking questions about school, going through your folders and your homework exercises, frowning and sighing out loud. She'd find Ms. Dallimore's essay and want to know why Neema hadn't even made a start.

"But—but she was only here in July!"

Neema's mum tried to hide a smile. "Not your gran. Nani."

"Nani?"

"Your great-grandmother," said Dad. "Mum's gran. Or, if you like, your gran's mum." His eyes shone beneath their sandy lashes; he loved anything having to do with families.

Because he never had one when he was little, Neema realized suddenly: no mum or dad, or aunts and uncles and cousins, no one at all except Sister Josephine and her little band of nuns, and the other orphans at the children's home. Perhaps that was why he loved her and Mum so much, so specially, loved even stern headmistress Gran. And now this other person, Nani.

"Remember when we went to Nani's place?" he asked her. "That little town beside the river? Remember the buffalos?"

Neema shook her head. No matter how many times she told him, Dad never quite believed that she didn't remember a thing about their trip to India, when she was only three. The trip to family, she thought.

"And how we used to sleep out on the roof at night, because it was so hot?" Her dad's voice became very soft and tender. "And go down to the river after tea? Remember the river, Neema?"

She didn't, of course. Not the river, anyway. But deep down in her memory, something began to stir. Neema screwed her eyes up, concentrating, and a picture of two old ladies floated slowly into her mind. Two old ladies standing side by side. "I think I do remember something," she said slowly, "only it might be a dream, because there's two old ladies, one in a white sari, and one in—a sort of rainbow one. A really bright rainbow."

Her mum and dad began to laugh.

"What's the matter? What's so funny?"

"You're remembering Nani—she's the one in the white sari—but you're also remembering Sumati, for sure."

"Who's Sumati?" asked Neema, bewildered.

"Your nani's friend. She always wears very bright saris—as a kind of celebration, ever since her husband ran away to be a Holy Man."

"Huh?"

"Great swirls of color," said Dad, grinning. "Riots of it! Pink and orange and purple and black and green—"

"Violent colors," murmured Neema's mum.

But Priya wished Sumati were coming too, so Nani would have someone to keep her company. Priya would take time off from her work at the university, of course, but what would she and Nani do all day?

"What will we *do* with her?" she asked aloud.

"Do with her?" Neema's dad sounded puzzled.

"How will we, sort of, entertain her, while she's here? Find things for her to do?"

"There's lots of things," said Neema eagerly. "We can take her to the beach—"

"That's just what I mean. We can't go there, she'd be shocked."

"Shocked?"

"Yes! All those skimpy swimsuits, and those, um, courting couples—"

"Oh." Neema's dad went pink. "Well, there's always the river; we can have a barbecue."

"No, we can't; she's a vegetarian, remember? We can't even walk by the river, the whole place smells of roasting meat! And that's another thing—we'll all have to be vegetarians while Nani's here."

"Fine with me," said Dad. "We can be vegetarians, can't we, Neema?"

"Sure." Neema forked up a thick slice of bacon from her plate.

"How does Nani spend her time when she's at home?" asked Dad. "What does she like to do?"

Priya cast her mind back to those childhood vacations she'd spent at Nani's house. Oh, how she'd hated that place! It was so hot, always, the sun blazing from the fierce blue sky, and there was nothing to do—not unless you wanted to walk by the river or along the dusty paths through the fields. She could hardly believe her own clever headmistress mother had grown up in such a place.

But how had Nani and Sumati spent their time? Little images rose up in her mind: the bazaar in the early morning; baskets of vegetables, the old ladies' long fingers testing the freshness of *bhindi* and *brinjal* and bitter gourd; the shady courtyard of the house, the two of them hunched over trays of rice and lentils, cleaning, sifting, cleaning again; the dark little kitchen shack, the smell of charcoal …

"She cooks," said Priya.

Neema's dad looked round their own bright kitchen. "Plenty of room to cook here."

"Yes, but—" Priya frowned. Obviously he didn't remember Nani's cooking, the cooking she'd learned from Sumati, and Sumati had learned from her old grandmother in that village in the hills. Priya shuddered at the thought of it: *rotis* you could sole your boots with, vegetables boiled in oil . . .

"But what?"

"Oh, nothing," answered Priya. They would soon find out. "Nani doesn't speak any English, remember. And you two don't speak a word of Hindi."

"But *you* do."

Priya flushed. "You know what Mum said about my Hindi last time she was here. She said I'd picked up such an awful accent she could hardly understand me."

That was just like Gran, thought Neema. Always criticizing.

"She said it sounded like a different language altogether, a really awful one, that should be called Hindian, or Australi."

"Oh well, your mother's a little—"

"Bossy," finished Neema.

"But if she can't make out my Hindi, then how will Nani?"

"Look, don't worry," said Neema's dad cheerfully. "We'll manage. Everything will be fine, you'll see." He smiled delightedly at his wife and daughter. "She's your grandmother, and Neema's *great*-grandmother; Nani's"—his voice lingered lovingly on the last word—"family."

Ms. Dallimore at Home

"My nani's coming to visit us from India," Neema told Kate as they walked down the corridor to Mr. Crombie's history lesson.

"Your gran?" replied Kate, a little startled. "But she was only here last winter."

Kate was afraid of Neema's gran: she looked at you so sternly. She looked at you as if she were about to ask you to spell the kind of word you'd never heard before, which only ever appeared in tiny print, in the deepest pages of the dictionary.

Neema giggled. "No, not Gran. Nani is *Mum's* gran; she's my great-grandmother."

"Your great-grandmother!" Kate had never met a great-grandmother before. "What's she like?"

Neema shook her head. "I don't remember. But she wouldn't be all headmistressy like Gran. Mum says Nani never even went to school."

"Half her luck," sighed Kate.

What would Nani be like? wondered Neema. Already Mum had prepared a room for her, the spare bedroom down the hall from Neema's. She'd bought a new duvet for the bed, and new curtains for the big window that overlooked the street and their front yard. In less than a week, Nani would be here.

Outside the library, Ivy Stevenson and her boyfriend, Danny Moss, were making plans for their evening. "Eight o'clock?" asked Danny.

Ivy nodded.

"Meet you on the corner of her street, then. And remember to wear dark clothes."

"Right," said Ivy, and then she nudged his arm. "Look! There she is!"

Ms. Dallimore was walking across the courtyard. Her step was light and brisk, her eyes sparkled, her pale face held the glow of great enthusiasm. Last night her dear companion, Vladimir, had given her the most marvelous topic for a senior essay: "The World, the Flesh, and the Devil." Her Year Tens had been getting a little sluggish lately, and Ms. Dallimore could hardly wait to try it out on them.

"She's getting paler," whispered Ivy.

"Paler and paler," responded Danny.

It was like a little song, a chant, that echoed everywhere around the school.

—

It was eight o'clock and Ms. Dallimore and Vladimir were dining by candlelight. It was a single candle, and a very small one—the sort you find on birthday cakes—because Vladimir's eyes were very sensitive to the light. He wore dark glasses inside the house and out, even on the gloomiest days of winter when the sun hadn't shone for weeks. Vladimir and Ms. Dallimore dined by candlelight and washed up by candlelight and listened to music in the dark. (Television was far too glary for Vladimir.)

Ms. Dallimore (whose name was Madeleine) smiled tenderly at her companion across their ill-lit table. He was wearing his painting smock with the big pockets, which he always wore at mealtimes, and washed all by himself, thoughtfully, to save Ms. Dallimore the bother.

"Some wine, my love?" asked Vladimir.

"Um, no," said Ms. Dallimore quickly, placing her hand across her glass. "I've got marking to do this evening."

Vladimir brewed his own wine from an old family recipe. He brewed it in the cellar, a place Ms. Dallimore never visited because it was so very black and creepy down there, and the stairs were so steep and frightening. The wine was a very deep dark red, almost black, with a strange taste that was almost—Ms. Dallimore shuddered—meaty.

"Cold, my love?" enquired Vladimir.

"What? Oh, no, no."

"Perhaps, as they say, a goose walked over your grave."

"A goose?" Ms. Dallimore sounded startled.

"Pardon, my Madeleine." Vladimir sighed. "Often I forget

I am no longer in Europe. Here it would be a magpie, or perhaps a crow."

"A crow," echoed Ms. Dallimore uneasily, forking up a piece of lamb chop and some peas. She glanced across at her companion"s plate, where the food lay quite untouched. Vladimir ate in the strangest way: one moment his plate would be full, but when you glanced again it would be almost empty.

"Oops!" In the gloom, Ms. Dallimore dropped her fork. When she came back from the kitchen with a clean one, Vladimir's chop and peas were gone; only his potatoes remained, right in the center of the plate.

Ms. Dallimore sat down.

"And how are 7B, Madeleine?" asked Vladimir.

"Oh! Oh dear! Vladimir, when I was in teachers' college, I had such dreams, such ideals! I thought I might encourage children to use their minds, their imaginations, to listen to the heavenly music of their souls …" Ms. Dallimore, seeking sympathy, gazed into Vladimir's dark glasses and saw only her own face mirrored there. She loved him dearly, but—"Vlad, isn't there something you can do about your glare problem? So you don't have to wear dark glasses all the time? And so we could"—she waved at the shadowy corners of the room—"have a little light in here?"

Vladimir sighed. "I fear not. Mine is a hereditary affliction, about which nothing can be done."

"But Vladimir, surely, in this day and age—"

"Ah! 'In this day and age,'" repeated Vladimir. "that sounds like a good title for one of your essays, my love. Or even, simply, 'Day and Age.'"

"Why, yes!" Ms. Dallimore exclaimed excitedly. "It—it's wonderful, Vladimir. "Day and Age"—why, they could write about almost anything." In her enthusiasm, Ms. Dallimore dropped her fork again, as Vladimir had known she would, and when she returned from the kitchen, the pockets of his smock were bulging and the potatoes on his plate were gone …

Outside the window, Ivy Stevenson and Danny Moss crouched among the bushes, trying to catch a glimpse of their Year Seven teacher's mysterious boyfriend. It was difficult because the room was so dark, full of flickering shadows from that single tiny candle. Dimly they could make out Ms. Dallimore's pale face, but her companion's back was turned toward them.

"Can you see him?" whispered Ivy.

Danny shook his head. "Nah."

And then, almost as if he'd heard them, Vladimir swung round in his chair to face the window.

Ivy and Danny saw a long white face beneath a shock of thick black hair; they saw full wet ruby lips and the spooky gleam of Vladimir's dark glasses.

"Geez, he's wearing shades in the middle of the night!"

"Oooh, look at his mouth, his lips are really red, like—like blood!"

Danny grabbed Ivy's hand. They scrambled from the

bushes and ran—ran with their hearts thudding, across the lawn to the gate, out into the street, down the road, and they didn't stop till they'd rounded two corners and were hidden in the prickly safety of old Mrs. Peterson's hedge.

"Think he saw us?"

"Nah—too dark."

"He might be able to see in the dark. It's the light that bothers them."

They crouched together, listening. After a few more minutes Danny said, "He's not coming after us, anyway. There's no footsteps."

"He mightn't *have* footsteps."

"Ah, come on!" said Danny. "Let's go down the reserve."

"Do you think he is?" asked Ivy a few moments later as they hurried on through the streets. "Do you think he really is—"

"Count Dracula?" Danny thought for a moment. "He does look a bit like him, with that spooky white face, and those shades—"

"And those lips," Ivy shivered.

"Except," said Danny, "Count Dracula's not—"

"Not real," finished Ivy, with a little sigh.

"Yeah. He's only someone from a fairy story. Know what? I reckon it's all coincidence, see?"

"Coincidence?"

"That Ms. Dallimore goes out with some weird guy who happens to look like a vampire, and that she's so pale. Red-haired people *are* pale."

"And getting paler," whispered Ivy.

"She's probably got some kind of vitamin deficiency."

"Iron," said Ivy knowledgeably, "or maybe B-12."

They walked on a little farther. "He's handsome, but," said Ivy.

"Handsome? That weirdo? You think so?"

"Sort of—distinguished. Romantic."

"Romantic!" scoffed Danny, but a moment later he put his arm around her. "Hey, Ive, guess what?"

"What?"

"I've found this really romantic place that no one else knows about. How about we go there one day?"

Ivy smiled. "Where is it?"

"The zoo."

"The *zoo*?" Ivy wrinkled her nose.

"Not *in* the zoo, exactly. You know that bushy bit, down behind the monkeys' enclosure? Well, there's a track through there, right down the hill to the beach at the bottom, and round the rocks there's this other little beach, really small—a sort of secret beach. It's got this great sand, really white, and sort of, uh—pearly."

"Pearly," echoed Ivy.

"So, wanna go there one day?"

"I might," replied Ivy. And then she sighed, because somehow she couldn't imagine Ms. Dallimore's distinguished companion taking a lady anywhere near a zoo.

Ms. Dallimore woke suddenly in the very middle of the

night. She pictured Vladimir's dinner plate as it had been the first time she'd gone out to the kitchen in search of a fresh fork: she saw the untouched chop, and the potatoes, and the peas. She remembered how when she'd come back the peas and the chop had vanished, and when she'd come back the second time the potatoes had gone too—the plate was bare. Completely bare.

The question was—and it worried Ms. Dallimore a little, as such things do in the middle of the night—what had happened to the chop bone?

·
·
·
·
·

"Is That Your Homework?"

"Is that your homework? Is it?"

Kate sat at her desk and Lucy hung over her shoulder, her warm breath tickling the back of her sister's neck.

"Yes," said Kate shortly. She'd hardly done a thing: only printed the title and begun to circle it with a border of bright green ivy leaves.

Lucy pointed a stubby finger at the words inside the leaves. "What does that say?"

"'Who Am I?'"

"Is that what you have to do? Write about who you are? Is it?"

"Yes."

"I could do that! It's easy!"

"You can't write."

"But when I can, when I go to Big School, next year, I'll write heaps and heaps. About me! About who I am!"

She would too, thought Kate.

"I can write my name—nearly. I can write 'L' for Lucy." A chubby hand reached out toward the box of pastels. Kate pushed it away.

"Don't touch! You know you're not allowed to use them! They're my special ones!"

For once Lucy didn't argue, but she kept on standing there, close up beside Kate's chair. Why did Lucy always have to *follow* her? Ten minutes ago Lucy had been in the kitchen, pestering Mum to take her to the zoo. A bout of pestering from Lucy could go on for hours, yet the moment Kate sat down at her desk to *think*, here she was again.

"You've hardly done *anything*!"

"That's because I've only just started," said Kate, struggling to keep her temper down. "I'm making the heading look nice, see?" She reached for the green pastel, to finish her ivy leaves.

It wasn't there.

"Where's my green pastel?"

Lucy's hands were hidden behind her back.

"Did you take it? Did you?"

"No!" Lucy held her hands out, empty. "It's there!" She pointed to the desk. Kate's crayon had rolled behind her pencil case.

"Oh." Kate picked it up and drew more leaves around her heading.

Lucy watched. "Now are you going to start writing? Writing about who you are?"

Kate's scalp began to itch, as it often did when Lucy started to annoy her.

"Are you? *Now?*"

Kate scratched wildly at her head. "In a minute. But I can't do it with you standing there watching me; I can't think when you do that. Why don't you go somewhere else?"

"Mum told me to come up here."

Kate clenched her teeth. Trust Mum.

"It's my room too," said Lucy. "Half of it is mine."

"You go over there, then," said Kate. "Play with your Noah stuff." She pointed to a far corner of the room, where the ark and its little plastic animals lay scattered on the floor.

Lucy stomped toward it. "You're *mean!* That's what you should write! 'My name is Katie and I'm *mean!*'"

Kate didn't answer. She bent her head over her desk.

"Make notes of your thoughts," Ms. Dallimore had told them. "Do it quickly, before they fly away. That will get you started." But what if you didn't have any thoughts, let alone flying ones? Kate chewed grimly on her pen.

"Look! Look, Katie!"

"What?"

Lucy was back by the chair, the tiny figure of Mrs. Noah clutched in her hand.

"See how she's got no head? Guess what happened? Mrs. Lion said to Mr. Lion, 'I'm feeling very hungry, darling, because I'm going to have a cub.' And then Mr. Lion said, 'Don't be sad, my dear. I know where there's a most delicious lady—'" Lucy planted a foot on the rung of her sister's chair, and swung on it. "And then—"

"Get off!" roared Kate. "You'll tip the chair over!"

"No, I won't! You're sitting in it, and you're so big and fat it can't fall down."

Kate pushed her off and got up from the desk. She marched to the door.

"Where are you going?" demanded Lucy.

"To the bathroom. At least I can be private there."

Kate sat on the edge of the bath and daydreamed about her half-completed room out on the back verandah. She imagined it all finished and ready for her—pictured the windows in place, the floor polished, a rug put down and curtains hung, her bed along one wall, her desk against the other—she imagined privacy and peace, and falling asleep without the sound of Lucy snoring.

When she'd calmed down she went back to her real room, and Lucy was still there. She was lying on her bed with her eyes closed, but Kate could tell from the tiny glimmer beneath her lashes that she was still awake.

Kate sat down at her desk and at once she saw that something funny had happened there. It was so very odd that for a moment Kate couldn't quite take it in. And then she did. Her pastels—her beautiful, special pastels that Aunty Marie had bought her from the art shop—were laid out in a long neat line beneath her workbook. And every single one of them had been neatly broken in half.

"Lucy!"

Lucy's eyes snapped open.

"Did you do this?"

Lucy nodded.

"You wicked, wicked—" *Girl* was too nice a word for Lucy. "You wicked little *pest!*"

Lucy began to sob. "I was helping you!"

"*Helping?*"

"Yes! Now you've got two of all of them. If you lose one, like you thought you'd lost the green one, then you've got an extra—"

Kate rushed to the door. "Mum!" she bellowed down the hallway. "Mum! Mum! Mum!"

It was late. Kate lay listening to Lucy snoring. Like an engine ticking over, she thought, stoking up for a fresh new day. "I hate that sound," Kate whispered to herself. "I hate it more than any other sound in the world." She glanced across at her sleeping sister. "And I hate *her.*"

All at once she remembered what Molly Matthews had said on the day Ms. Dallimore had handed out their essay topic: how what you loved showed who you were.

And if that was true, then wouldn't it be the same with what you hated?

Kate slipped from her bed, grabbed her workbook, and hurried down the hall. The living room was empty: Mum and Dad had long since gone to bed. It was quiet and peaceful; the dark at the windows made Kate feel as if she had the whole world to herself.

She opened her workbook and picked up her pen. "I am a person who hates my little sister," she began, and then, beneath the garlanded title, her pen began to *fly*. Across the page, and the next page, and the next—it was wonderful, marvelous. She could actually describe stuff, as she'd never been able to do before: like the way her scalp began to itch when Lucy got her *really* angry, as she'd done tonight, an itching that grew and grew until it was like the pricking of a thousand little knives …

It was two in the morning when her mother appeared at the door.

"Kate, what are you *doing*?"

Kate looked up with a dazzling smile. "I got an idea for my essay, and I wanted to write it down before I forgot, so I came down here." She added virtuously, "I didn't want to turn the bedroom light on in case that would wake Lucy up."

"Oh," said her mother, startled by the wild gleam in her daughter's eye. Mrs. Sullivan padded across the carpet in her old felt slippers and placed a cool hand on her daughter's forehead. It wasn't hot at all.

"Well, go to bed now," she told her. "It's very, very late and you've got school tomorrow."

"She was doing homework," Mrs. Sullivan told her husband a few minutes later, when she was sure Kate was safely tucked in bed. "At least that's what she said—I hope she's not coming down with something."

"She'll be all right," said Trevor Sullivan sleepily.

"Perhaps she's growing up, Trev."

Kate's dad sighed and turned over. "I'd better get on with that room of hers then—sometime soon."

"*Very* soon," said Mrs. Sullivan firmly.

Awkward

Neema lay on her bed thinking about the flying boy. She'd seen him again this afternoon; she'd glanced through the window halfway through music and there he was playing cricket on the oval with the Year Eight boys. The way he ran, with a long, loping stride, had seemed utterly familiar to her. Now she knew he was in Year Eight, only a year older than her. But she still didn't know his name and she didn't want to ask anyone. It could be embarrassing to ask the name of a boy at school.

Sheep, shepherd, lamb: if she could work out why those words kept coming into her head whenever she thought of him …

"Nirmolini?"

A small, wrinkled face peered round the edge of the door. A wisp of floaty white sari.

Nani!

Neema sat up quickly, pulling her skirt down over her knobbly knees.

Nani had been with them a whole week now, and she wasn't the least bit like bossy old Gran, but it was all sort of—awkward. How Neema wished she'd learned Hindi back when she was younger, as Mum and Dad had suggested. But it hadn't seemed important then. Why learn Hindi when Mum spoke English all the time, and Gran too, when she was here? Why waste every Saturday morning at the Indian Culture School, when there were so many other things you could do?

And now …

Nani stood in the doorway.

"*Soti ho kya?*" she asked Neema, making a small rocking motion with her hands.

That must mean "sleep," thought Neema. Nani must be asking if she'd been asleep.

"Oh, no, no," she said quickly, politely, the way she always spoke to Nani. "I wasn't asleep, you didn't wake me up or anything. I was just having a rest, lying here, thinking about, um …" She trailed off, hearing her own silly voice rattling round the room.

She was chattering again. She sometimes did that when she found herself alone with Nani—talked really fast, as if she couldn't stop, because she was embarrassed that she couldn't understand a word her great-grandmother said. And Nani kept trying to talk to her. Nani would try to tell her something and then stand there silently, waiting, as if she expected

Neema to reply. But how could she, when she didn't know what Nani had said and couldn't give any answer that Nani might understand? So Neema chattered on in English to fill the silence up.

There was a silence now.

Nani stood patiently a little way inside the room, her gaze fixed intently on her great-granddaughter's face. Studying it, thought Neema, as if her face was some kind of map and Nani was searching for a special landmark there. It made Neema long to run away—and then it made her feel mean, for wanting to.

Because Nani was lovely. She was gentle and kindly, and she loved all three of them; you could see it in her face. You could see it especially at dinnertime, now that Nani insisted on doing all their cooking—in the way she ladled her marvelous food onto their plates (Mum didn't think it was marvelous, but Dad and Neema did) and then watched while they ate it, as if giving food were a kind of love.

Neema sprang up and began to bustle round the room, picking things up and putting them away, a set stern expression on her face, as if she were very busy and had important stuff to do. She went to the desk and shuffled the folders there, and her great-grandmother followed her, two small steps behind. Nani pointed to the sheet of paper, still blank except for Neema's name and the title of Ms. Dallimore's essay.

"*Iskool ka kaam*?" she asked.

Neema could tell it was a question because Nani's voice went up a little at the end. "It's homework," she replied.

"Kaisa kaam?"

Now she must be asking what kind of homework it was, like Gran did when she came to visit; only Nani's voice wasn't bossy like Gran's, it was soft and rather shy.

"For English. It's an essay." Neema's voice sped up again. "Well, it's not an essay yet, because I haven't really started it. No one has, except Kate, and she's actually finished hers. Can you believe that? *Kate!* And it's the kind of essay where it's really hard to think of anything to say. Like, I don't know—" Neema broke off on a sudden gasp, and Nani stood there, still studying her face.

Neema smiled uncertainly, and then Nani studied the smile, frowning slightly, as if there was something wrong with it, as if it was the wrong sort of smile.

It was. Neema could see her face reflected in the closet mirror, a face that hardly looked like hers. Her mouth was a stiff, quirky shape, and her little dimple didn't show. Oh, how she wished Nani would leave her alone!

And as if she'd heard that very thought Nani turned away sadly and walked out through the door.

Gone.

Neema stood and listened to the soft brushing sound of Nani's bare feet on the polished boards of the hall. "Nani!" she called guiltily, running after her.

Nani turned round.

"Good night," said Neema. "Good night, Nani."

Good night. Kalpana knew those words. Indeed, she knew many English words that she'd picked up from Usha, long ago when her daughter was small and had gone to the English Language School. But she couldn't bring herself to say them out loud to other people; she was afraid they might sound thick and stupid in her voice. That people might laugh ...

"You are too proud, always," Sumati often said, "too proud in little things." And she was, thought Kalpana. Too proud to risk one single word, even to her lovely great-granddaughter, Nirmolini.

"*Soja beti*," she said instead, which meant, though Neema didn't know it, "Sleep well, my child."

Was that good night? wondered Neema. Should she repeat it, then? But what if it meant something else? Like, "Go away, you heartless girl!" Or what if it was a phrase that, in India, only old people were allowed to use?

So Neema only smiled again, that stiff, uncertain smile she always gave to Nani, which froze her soft features and concealed the small dimple that showed when she truly smiled.

Dear Sumati

My dear Sumati, wrote Kalpana.

I am happy to hear that you have arrived safely at your sister's place after the long train journey from Ahmedabad and those many troublesome hours on the bus.

Yes, you are right: some of these bus drivers are ignorant fellows indeed! To think that he would boss you around: refuse to let you take your sack of sweet potatoes onto the bus—the sweet potatoes you bought for your sister Lakshmi from Ratan Lal's stall! Everyone knows that Ratan Lal's sweet potatoes are the best in all India, perhaps even in the world. That this bus driver should throw them on the roof rack! And that later, in the mountains, you would look out through the window and see them tumbling down! And hear the other travelers cry out in distress, believing your potatoes were stones and avalanche!

I am not surprised to learn your throat is sore from shouting (take lemon and best honey, mixed together, warm), and yes, you may be right again: that driver may have been a schoolteacher in his former life, and for his sins will surely be a cockroach in the next.

Here it is very strange, Sumati, so strange it would take many pages to tell. The city is as big as Delhi, and yet the street where my granddaughter and her family live is empty in the middle of the afternoon! And at night, Sumati—at night it is so quiet you would not believe! At home, even at the latest hour, there is always some small sound to remind you that you are among other humans on this earth: the rumble of an oxcart on its way to market, the chatter of late travelers passing by, a little snatch of film-song from the rickshaw wallahs' camp at the bottom of the road …

Kalpana put down her pen and walked to the window, drawing the curtain aside. The street outside lay still and silent; nothing moved except for a large white fluffy cat stealthily crossing the road. As Kalpana watched he leapt onto the gate-post and began to clean himself, then raised his head to stare at her with big round yellow eyes.

"A cat," said Kalpana, out loud in English. It was the first English word she had really learned, printed in big letters in her little daughter's first English primer. They'd learned it together, all three of them, she and Sumati and Usha, on the verandah back home, long, so long ago.

Kalpana's gaze drifted to the big tree in the garden, whose branches spread over the low, flat roof of the garage. She'd known the moment she saw the tree that it was the same as the ones she'd seen in her flying dream: it was the same gray silvery color and had the same long thin pointed leaves. "A gum tree," Priya had told her, and in the streets of this suburb there were many gum trees, and somewhere, Kalpana knew, there would be a lake like the one in her dream with a bank of the silvery trees alongside.

Now there was a sound from the street. Faintly, in the distance, she heard a soft rhythmic clicking noise: tick-tock, tick-tock, tick-tock—what could it be? The sound grew louder, the white cat sprang from its post and ran away, and there, by the glow of the streetlight, Kalpana saw a tall, thin boy sailing past the house, so fast he seemed to fly.

She blinked and rubbed her eyes. When she looked again the boy was gone. Perhaps she'd dreamed him, though as she listened, she could still hear that faint tick-tocking, growing softer and softer until it was swallowed into the thick silence of the foreign night. "*Uran khatola*," she whispered. And then, more slowly, as she worked the English words out, "The—the flying boy!"

I have been having that flying dream again, she wrote on to Sumati. *You know, the one you laughed about, where I was flying, faster and faster, but only a simple hand's height above the ground. But you didn't laugh, my dear Sumati, when I told you the feeling of my dream: how if I flew fast enough, I would see my dear Raj's face again; I would see his special smile …*

Gull Oliver skimmed along the moonlit street, heading back to his home on Delphi Drive.

That had been *her* house back there; he was certain of it

now. He remembered that big gum tree, the way it leaned a little, spreading its branches over the flat roof of the garage. Back at Short Street Primary, Mrs. Flannery had made sure all the Grade One kids who'd been chosen as shepherds knew the houses where their lambs lived—"Just in case," she'd said.

Nirmolini's mum had asked him to tea: he remembered the chocolate cake, and Nirmolini sitting beside him at the table, and Mrs. Grace asking him about his name, like people often did. They always thought it had to do with birds.

"It's Gulliver, really," he'd explained.

"Gulliver? Like the book?"

He'd nodded. "It's because Mum had me on her travels."

"Oh," Mrs. Grace had murmured. A bit shocked, Gull thought now, though he hadn't realized that, back when he was six. And he remembered how Nirmolini, sitting beside him, had said, "It's a good name, Gulliver."

And all that had been seven whole years ago. Wasn't seven a magic number? And there *was* something magical about meeting a girl you'd last seen when she was five, who'd changed like a princess in a fairy tale, so that approaching her house Gull had expected it would be Nirmolini standing in that lighted window, like Rapunzel in her tower or Sleeping Beauty in her silent castle.

But the face he'd seen there, though he fancied it had a tiny look of Nirmolini, had been very, very old. Her gran, Gull supposed as he swirled into his driveway, where his mum was waiting at the door.

"I wish you wouldn't go out skating late at night," she grumbled.

"Late? It's only nine-thirty," he told her. "A perfectly respectable hour."

"Still—"

"Mum, it's magic skating at night along those empty streets. You feel the whole world might be yours!"

"The whole world!" But her lips curved into a smile.

"And it gives you these really amazing dreams! You should try it, Mum."

"Oh, come *on*!" She punched him lightly on the shoulder. "Look at me." She patted her big fat front. "I'd break your precious board in two! Though perhaps," she added dreamily, "one day …"

"One day," echoed Gull. "I'll take you up on that. You've made a promise, Mum."

A Spot of Writing

Blocky Stevenson was about to do a spot of writing. He wanted to get that thing of Ms. Dallimore's off his mind, where it hung like a drab black curtain over the better things in life. He wanted it out of the way by Saturday, so he could watch the footy game in peace. Out of the way and *done*. Kate Sullivan had hers all done, and if Kate Sullivan could do it, so could he. Then he'd be *free*.

First Blocky arranged his desk. He cleared everything off it—footy mags and crumpled sports pages, socks and jerseys, two mugs that had once held milk and now held mold, a plate with flaky crumbs of pastry and a smear of tomato sauce—and chucked the lot into the bottom of his closet.

Then he took a clean sheet of paper from his work folder and lined it up on the desk: nudging the edges with his big blunt fingers, getting them exactly straight.

Something was missing.

A pen.

Blocky rooted through his school bag, turning up odds and ends he hadn't seen for months. No pen. He took a bite from a battered old pear and wiped his fingers down his T-shirt.

"Mum!" he roared toward the family room, where his parents were watching TV. "Mum!"

"Yeah?" Mrs. Stevenson roared back.

"Do youse know where there's a pen?"

"A pen?" Mrs. Stevenson's roar was muted by surprise.

"Yeah!"

"There's one near the phone!"

Mrs. Stevenson turned to her husband. "He's looking for a *pen*. I think he might be going to do some homework."

Mr. Stevenson grunted. He thought there might be other uses for a pen, at least in Blocky's case. "Probably wants to clean his ears."

Blocky thumped down the hall toward the telephone. He grabbed the pen and took it to his room.

The sheet of paper had got skewed; Blocky lined up the edges again, smearing them with pear.

"Geez!" He crumpled the paper and wiped his fingers more thoroughly down his front; then he took a new sheet, lined it up, and settled down.

WHO AM I? he began to print, but the ink ran out before he reached the "M."

"Mum!"

"Yeah?"

"This pen doesn't work!"

"Find another one, then!"

"Where?"

"Kitchen drawer!"

"Which one?"

"I don't know, love. Just look around. Your dad and me are trying to watch this cooking show."

Cooking show! That was a laugh, thought Blocky as he headed down the hall. Some clown must be showing the pair of them a new way to open cans ...

There were lots of drawers in the kitchen, and Blocky tried them all.

No pens.

Just a couple of old topless markers, all dried up.

The back door banged open and his sister Ivy burst into the room. "What are you up to?" she said in greeting.

"Looking for a pen."

"A *pen*?"

"Yeah. What's so funny about that? I can write, you know. Hey, can you lend me one?"

"No way. You ruined the last one."

"Go on."

"You're not mucking up another pen of mine."

"Have a heart!"

"No! They're all at school anyway."

"Bet they're not," said Blocky, and in his chest, beneath the grubby pear-stained T-shirt, he felt a pang of hurt, the same kind of pang he got when Mr. Crombie called him

Leatherbrain. "I've got feelings, you know," he muttered. But Ivy didn't seem to hear him; she simply pointed to the cupboard under the sink and said, "There might be one in there." Then she left the room.

"Is that you, Ivy?" yelled her mother as Ivy's boots passed loudly by the door.

"Yeah."

"How was the Girls' Friendly Society?"

"Friendly."

Mrs. Stevenson didn't know quite what to make of that. She had a niggling feeling that Ivy hadn't gone to the old church hall.

But Ivy had gone there. She'd walked in the front door, past those losers in their unbelievable blue skirts and blouses, out the back, and down the path to the reserve, and Danny. They'd talked about Danny's secret romantic place, the beach down below the zoo. They were going there a week from Friday, when Wentworth had a half vacation. They'd talked for ages, and, well … now Ivy's curls were mussed and her new top was on back to front. Blocky hadn't noticed, but her mother would. Ivy hurried to her room and slammed the door.

Blocky opened the cupboard underneath the sink. It was full of old ice cream containers and plastic bags, but right at the back, in a very dark corner, Blocky's sharp eyes found something else. Not a pen, but—

"Yeah!" Blocky punched his fist in the air. His old junior football, the one Pops had given him when he was six! Blocky reached in a long arm and grabbed it, scattering plastic bags.

He hadn't seen it for years, yet it was still firm and filled with air, almost as good as new.

Ms. Dallimore's essay lost its hold on him. She mightn't even be at Wentworth when the thing was due—Ms. Dallimore was heading for a fall, for sure. All the kids in Year Eight said that the guy who picked her up from school in the big black car was Count Dracula.

Cradling the ball gently in his hands, Blocky lunged out through the door. He switched the floodlight on; light poured out over the yard, and through the windows of the family room.

Mrs. Stevenson got up and drew the curtains.

"What's he up to now?"

"Kicking a ball around." Mrs. Stevenson sighed.

"Looks like the homework didn't last."

Again Mrs. Stevenson sighed.

"He'll be right," promised Mr. Stevenson. "Blocky will. He's a good kid, and he's got—feelings."

The last word came out muffled, and Mrs. Stevenson turned to him with horror on her face. "*Feelers*? He's grown *Feelers*?"

"Nah," Mr. Stevenson chortled. "Feelings, that's what I said. Block's got *feelings*."

"Oh." Mrs. Stevenson considered this. "Yeah," she said at last. "Yeah, he has."

Outside in the yard, Blocky drew one huge foot back and aimed the ball against the wall. It bounced, he kicked it back, it bounced, he kicked again. Thud. Thud. Thud.

The house shuddered. His mum and dad hardly noticed, they were so used to it.

Mum's Going Loopy

Neema's mum stood outside the Indian video store, waiting for Nani to exchange her film. No, not exchange, *renew*, because Nani watched the same film over and over—an ancient, crackly Hindi movie, a tale of love lost and found and lost again. And Priya felt obliged to watch it with her, so many times that the plaintive theme song had burned into her brain, quite drowning out little Miss Dabke's heavenly mathematical music of the spheres.

She stared down at the shopping slumped against her feet: more pickles and spices from the Indian grocery, and a five-kilo bag of potatoes, because Nani was planning to make *khatta alu* for dinner.

Khatta alu! Priya shuddered. She'd hated that dish since she was a child: great chunks of potatoes fried in oil with aniseed. Neema and Ignatius would wolf it down enthusiastically; they *loved* Nani's cooking. While she, the Indian member of the family, would push it round and round her plate, Nani hovering over her, urging her to eat. "Eat, little one. You are too thin! Eat! Eat!"

Next to the potatoes sat a brimming bag of Priya's least favorite vegetable: eggplant. "Ugh! Yuk!" Priya groaned aloud, and a stern-faced man passing on the footpath stared at her in alarm.

Priya blushed. What was *happening* to her? Two short weeks ago, she'd been Professor Priya Grace, head of mathematics at the university. Now, she was like one of those squalling little kids you saw in Safeway, tugging at their mothers, bawling to go home. But she *did* want to go home. They'd spent *hours* in that Indian grocery, where Nani roamed contentedly, reading lists of ingredients from the backs of pickle jars.

"Nani!" she called.

Nani came out from the shop, beaming, the same old video tucked beneath her arm. She sang its theme song softly as they walked on up the street, and Priya sang along with her: "*Beloved! After so long, to see your dear face once more—*"

Why did such a sad song sound so oddly joyous? wondered Priya. "*Beloved! After so long—*" she warbled, and realized suddenly that she was singing by herself; Nani wasn't there beside her anymore. Priya whirled around and peered back down the street: Nani had come to a standstill outside the window of the sports store. Priya clicked her tongue irritably. What on earth could possibly interest her in there?

"What are you looking at?" she asked, coming up beside

her grandmother. "Those running shoes? Do you want to buy a present? For your nephews?"

But Nani's nephews would be grandfathers by now.

"Grandnephews? Great-grandnephews?"

Nani was silent.

Priya thought this was because Nani hadn't understood her awful Hindi. "A present for your great-grandnephews?" she repeated carefully.

Kalpana was silent because she was too embarrassed to tell her granddaughter how she wanted a pair of those young people's shoes for herself—and a pair for Sumati, of course. "Flying shoes," she called them, because she'd seen how people walked when they wore them: effortlessly, bouncily, as if they were floating on air. For young people, she'd thought, but then, yesterday, outside the grocery, she'd noticed an old woman—surely as old as herself—wearing the flying shoes.

"I am only looking," Kalpana told her granddaughter. And then she looked a little longer, while Priya tapped her foot and sighed. Kalpana looked long enough to choose the ones she liked best: white with blue triangles on their sides, like the ones her own Nirmolini wore. And the purple ones with orange laces for Sumati; Sumati would love those colors.

Priya grabbed her arm. "Come on, Nani, let's go home."

Always in a hurry, poor girl, thought Kalpana as she followed her granddaughter along the street toward the parking lot. She was exactly like her mother Usha: always fussing, always bossing, always rush rush rush.

—

"Mum's going loopy," Neema told Kate.

Kate nodded. Her mum went loopy sometimes too: when she worked late and came home to find that no one had taken the meat from the freezer to thaw. Or when Lucy did something really drastic ...

"Little loopy or big?" she asked Neema.

"Getting big."

"How come?"

"It's Nani—"

"But your nani's lovely." Kate had met her, and thought she'd never seen anyone so romantic-looking, even though she was so old. That floaty white sari! And those big dark shining eyes! Nani had given Kate an Indian sweet she'd made, called *ras malai*—it had tasted heavenly.

"I know she's lovely," Neema said, a little irritably. "But it's as if—oh, I don't know. Like she and Mum are these really different kinds of people, and Mum can't figure out how to entertain her."

Kate frowned. "Entertain her? How do you mean?"

"Oh, you know—keeping her company, finding things to do."

"What?" Now Kate's voice sounded almost cross. "But Nani's not a baby! It's only babies who have to be entertained! She's really ..."

"Clever" Kate had been about to say, only "clever" didn't seem quite the right word. Jessaline O'Harris was clever, lots of people were, but Kate had glimpsed something more than cleverness in Neema's great-grandmother's eyes, a quality for which she couldn't find the word. "She's special, she's got …" Kate paused again.

"Imagination," supplied Neema. Only last night her dad had told her this was the meaning of Kalpana, Nani's name.

"Yes," agreed Kate. "Like she'd be really interesting to talk to, if you only could. How come you don't know any Hindi? How come you didn't learn it from your mum?"

"Mum always speaks English at home, and when she wanted me to learn, well, I—" Neema was saved from further uncomfortable explanation because Kate wasn't listening anymore; she was waving to someone on the other side of the road.

Neema turned to look. And then to stare. She could feel her eyes growing big and round, and her mouth dropping open, just a tiny bit.

It couldn't be!

But it was: the boy on the skateboard, the flying boy, *her* flying boy.

"Hi!" Kate was calling, and "Hi!" the boy called back. And for a second, before he sailed away, Neema thought he smiled at *her*. But why should he? Of course the smile had been for Kate.

"Who's that?" she asked, trying to keep a tremble from her voice.

"Gull Oliver," replied Kate coolly. "He lives down at the bottom of our street. You know him."

"Me?" Neema felt her face grow hot. "No, I don't. I didn't even know his name."

"You've forgotten," said Kate. "Though I suppose he looked different back then."

"Back then?"

"At Short Street, when we were in Prep. Gull was in Grade One; then his dad got this job in Germany and they all went overseas. They came back only this year. Don't you remember him a little bit, though? You *should*."

"Why should I?"

"Remember Mrs. Flannery? The little kids' headmistress up at Short Street? And how she used to call the kids in Prep 'new lambs'?"

"New lambs!"

"Soppy, eh? But she was nice, Mrs. Flannery. And remember how she had this program for the first week where every kid in Prep had a special friend from Grade One to show them round and stuff?"

"And they were called shepherds!"

"That's right. Well, I had that awful Rosie Turner, but you—"

"Had Gull Oliver!"

"That's right. He was your shepherd." Kate grinned. "And you were his little new lamb."

Knobbly Knees

Of course! Gull Oliver had been her shepherd when she started primary school! Neema had been one of those weepy little kids who cried on their first day. She'd been standing at the window, all red and hot and teary, watching Mum walk away—down the path, through the gate, and round the corner, out of sight, away—when a voice said cheerfully, "Don't worry, she'll come back." She'd turned and found a bigger boy with curly hair, whose eyes crinkled at the corners when he smiled.

"When it's your first day you think they won't come back, but they *do*," he'd gone on calmly, handing her a crumpled tissue to dry her eyes. "I cried too, when I was new."

She remembered the cool, dry touch of his hand as he steered her along the corridors, pointing out the places she should know. "That's the art room, see? And the library. And the girls'—well, you know what—are over there. People say they're heaps cleaner than the boys' ones, but I wouldn't know 'cause I've never been in there."

He'd found Kate for her. "See that girl over there? The one with the frizzy hair? She looks nice, don't you think? I reckon she might make a really good friend for you."

Did Gull Oliver remember her from then? All red and hot and weepy, sticky …

Neema jumped up and went to look at herself in the big mirror on the closet door. The mirror showed a slender, long-legged girl, whose perfect oval face, with its large, lustrous eyes, was framed by a cloud of soft, dark shining hair.

Neema didn't see these lovely things. Her eyes were focused on what she hated most: her big knobbly ugly grotty sticking-out knees, so big they were like nasty bony faces jeering out at her. Dad said they weren't ugly, of course; and Mum kept on saying her legs would grow into them, very soon. Neema didn't believe them …

"Neema?" Her mum peered round the door. "Can you help Nani with the washing-up?"

"I've got all this homework. I've got this essay, Mum."

And that was true. Ms. Dallimore's essay—or was it Count Dracula's?—still lay untouched on the farthest corner of Neema's desk.

"Come on, now. It'll take only five minutes. I offered to help, but Nani wouldn't let me—it's you she really wants."

Dad's voice sounded from the hall. "She wants her only great-granddaugher, the beautiful Nirmolini"—his voice took on those Bible tones—"whose name is like perfume poured out—"

Neema went downstairs.

Kalpana loved everything about her Nirmolini. She loved her hands, so busy with the dish towel, square hands, a little like her own; she loved the way her hair grew, like Raj's had, in a springy arc from her broad forehead; she loved her strong young legs and the delicate ankles above the sturdy flying shoes.

She *would* buy those flying shoes in the window of the sports store, decided Kalpana. She'd buy them tomorrow, when she went out with Priya, and she'd get the purple ones for Sumati, too. Even if Priya laughed and said they were too old for flying shoes. Even if Priya was in a hurry and impatient, and Priya would be, because she was so like Usha. Usha had been rushy and impatient even when she was a little child. On summer evenings Kalpana and Sumati would go to the river. They did nothing there; they simply sat, dreamily watching the sky, or the water flowing by. Usha had hated that: ten minutes by the river and she wanted to rush away. And Priya had been just the same when she'd visited on vacations.

Nirmolini was different, thought Kalpana. Nirmolini would sit by the river with them. Hadn't she done so when she was a tiny child? Sat between her and Sumati, quietly, gazing up at the wide blue sky?

How small and delicate Nani was, thought Neema, and how

gracefully she moved. Standing beside her, Neema felt big and gawky, like the picture in that storybook she'd had when she was little—the one of the princess and her great big genie slave. There were no photographs of Nani when she was young, but Gran said she'd been very beautiful, and you could see a little bit of it even now, if you imagined the wrinkles away and changed the white hair to black. You could see it in the fine heart shape of her face and the softness of her eyes. Neema's mum was beautiful too, and on the book-shelf in her study there was a framed photograph of a lovely, gentle-looking girl that Neema often took down to examine, because who could believe that that sweet-faced girl was her stern headmistress gran?

Nani was looking at her, Neema noticed as she dried the dishes, studying her face in that way she had: gravely, carefully. Perhaps she was thinking, as Neema was herself, that her great-granddaughter was the plain one of the family. Nani's gaze drifted downward, and Neema wished she wasn't wearing shorts, because Nani was staring at her knobbly knees, and then at her new white air-soled running shoes, which made her feet look big. Nani probably disapproved of running shoes; old people often did.

Neema sighed and counted the cups and dishes on the sink. There weren't many left to wash; it would be only a few minutes longer before she could get away. At least Nani wasn't *talking* to her, telling her stuff and asking those ques-tions Neema couldn't understand.

At that very moment, as if once again she'd read her great-granddaughter's thoughts, Nani spoke.

"Do you remember the river, Nirmolini?" Kalpana asked in Hindi. "Do you remember the river in my town?"

Neema's face stiffened; the anxious smile that hid her true expression tightened at her lips. What had Nani asked her? The question had her name in it; that was all she knew. It could have been anything. It could have been something like, "I wonder how you will ever find a husband, poor Nirmolini, when you have such ungainly knobbly knees? And such huge feet, in those ugly, clumsy shoes?"

It probably was, thought Neema, panicking suddenly, because now Nani was looking at her again, and there was a tiny frown between her eyebrows, as if something made her sad.

In her soft, sweet Hindi, Kalpana asked once more, "The river, Nirmolini? Where you sat with Sumati and me?"

Neema froze. She was saying it again! Or something like it—because one of the words was the same. *Nadi. Nadi* could mean gawky, or even ugly; it sounded like it might. Nani thought Neema was a *nadi* girl. She'd mentioned Sumati's name too—she was probably saying how Sumati would also wonder, shaking her head sadly when she received the letter that told her how Neema had grown up very plain. And worse than plain: *nadi.*

"In the evenings, all three of us?" asked Nani softly. "You used to love the river, and the sky."

Nadi! There it was again. Neema flushed, and tears welled in her eyes. "I—I have to go and do my homework!" she stammered, and tossing the dish towel onto the bench, she ran out from the room.

How stupid I am! Kalpana scolded herself. She had upset Nirmolini, made her feel awkward, as she always did, chattering on in words the poor child didn't understand. And Kalpana actually knew the English word for *nadi*, of course she did. It was "river." And she knew "in my town." She should have spoken them, even if she said them wrong, even if she couldn't manage a whole sentence but only "River in my town?" She heard Sumati's voice again: "Too proud in little things!"

Kalpana picked up the dish towel and folded it slowly, carefully: it was still warm, still warm from Nirmolini's little hands.

·
·
·
·
·
•

$\mathcal{T}rouble$ $\mathcal{S}leeping$

My dear Sumati, wrote Kalpana.

I am sorry to hear your throat is once again quite sore from shouting. It's a pity that your sister's goat has made it his business to become your enemy, and that he should discover your two best saris spread out on the bushes to dry. What trials you have in life! Try not to worry too much about the saris. When we are both back home, we will go to the bazaar and buy the best and brightest saris in Bhairon Singh's shop. As we both know, he is the only person in the whole of India who understands how to make rainbows out of cloth.

In the meantime, keep up the honey and lemon—once in the morning, and again at night. And dear Sumati, do try to stop shouting. Speak softly to the goat, in sweet and gentle words.

Ah, words, Sumati! I think of you often at your sister's place—of you and Lakshmi talking together, the words flowing easily between you, clear as soft new rain.

Here words are muddy for me. The little awkward English that we learned when Usha was at school I am too proud to speak. Remember how Usha and her friends giggled when they heard us in the courtyard, "practicing"? And remember how we also laughed, thinking it strange that such funny, unfamiliar sounds could ever tell of anything we knew?

But here, those words we found so funny are meaning everything.

*My great-granddaughter says only "*Namaste.*" She says it perfectly, of course—but that is all.*

My son-in-law is a kind and loving man, but I think, like me, he has no ease with foreign tongues. When he tries a word (and he does try; he is less proud than me), his face grows the shade of carrots, those young tender carrots we buy in the bazaar at springtime, to make fresh pickles and Gajjar Karrah.

Priya, of course, speaks Hindi, but it is a strange kind of Hindi now, Sumati. You cannot say her tongue is heavy because she speaks fast, very fast—she was always a nervous child. And her words have that strange "yoing yoing" sound the people's tongues make here—often I cannot make out what she says.

It is my great-granddaughter I would like to understand, and talk with. If only I were not—

Kalpana laid down her pen and went to the window. It was time, she knew, for the flying boy to come past the house; already she could hear that faint tick-tocking in the distance, far away down the street.

Gull Oliver stopped outside the gate to look up at the house. The streetlight shone on him; Kalpana saw his feet in big white flying shoes, and beneath them, the wooden board with wheels on which he stood. She had seen such things in the window of the sports store: skateboards, they were called. "Ah," she murmured, as she raised her hand to wave at him. The boy waved back, and then Kalpana watched him sail away down the street, faster and faster, as if he were flying, a simple hand's height from the ground.

Gull's route homeward took him past the house where Ms. Dallimore lived. It was a creepy house, thought Gull, tall and narrow, with two crooked chimney pots, its whole front veiled by a thick net of glistening ivy. The windows were shuttered and dark. Gull skated by as quickly as he could.

Could there be any truth in that story the Year Eight kids whispered round the school? That Ms. Dallimore—Oh, get real, he told himself; of course it wasn't true. All kinds of weird yarns went round about the teachers: how Mr. Crombie had been in the local paper because he had two wives and fifteen children; how Mrs. Tierny had been taken to court for slipping a live ferret into her neighbor's mailbox; how the headmaster had a weekend job as a children's party clown—they couldn't *all* be true.

Ms. Dallimore was simply unusual. She was the kind of teacher you remembered, like his mum remembered Mr. Glazby, who'd jump up on his desk, arms waving, to recite a favorite poem.

"Nirmolini, oh Nirmolineee—" he caroled as he swooped into his drive. His sharp-eared mother heard him from inside the house, and smiled. Now where had she heard that name before? Because she had heard it, Mrs. Oliver felt sure, somewhere, a long time ago.

"Nirmolini …" she whispered as she lay awake that night. "Joe!" she said, prodding Gull's father awake. "Joe, listen!"

"What?" Mr. Oliver mumbled sleepily.

"I've worked out who Nirmolini is!"

"Nirmolini? What's that?"

"It's a girl's name, a name Gull keeps on—sort of singing."

"Yeah?"

"She's that little girl Gull used to shepherd."

"Shepherd?"

"When he was in Grade One at Short Street, before we went away? Remember how they had that program where the Grade One kids looked after the Preps? She was that little dark-haired girl who came here once, to tea?"

"Ur, right," said Mr. Oliver foggily. "Yeah, nice little kid she was."

Nirmolini would be quite grown up by now, thought Mrs. Oliver. And—and beautiful, perhaps.

In her creepy house, Ms. Dallimore was also having trouble sleeping. "Vladimir! Vlad! Wake up!"

Vladimir's hooded eyes sprang open instantly. "Madeleine?"

"I've had the most awful nightmare, Vlad!"

"A nightmare, my love? Of what?"

She drew a long, shaky breath. "I dreamed this old, old Indian woman was standing right *there!*" Ms. Dallimore's fine green eyes were glassy with fright as she pointed to a spot beside the bed. "Oh, Vlad! She was a perfect *crone!* In the most hideous sari, all clashing colors—violet and orange and puce—and she was *hissing* at me, Vlad!"

"Hissing, my love?"

"Violently! Her name was Sumati."

"She told you her name?"

"No! I just *knew* it. This was a dream, Vlad." Ms. Dallimore glanced nervously toward the side of the bed where Sumati had appeared. "Or at least I hope it was!"

"And what did this ancient Oriental lady have to say?"

"That was the worst part; she *accused* me!"

"Accused you?" For a moment Vladimir seemed uneasy. "Of what?"

"Of—of being bossy to children."

"Ah." Vladimir smiled.

"Of—cudgeling their brains!"

"Truly?"

"Truly. Vlad, do you think I cudgel children's brains?"

"Of course not. They have no brains to cudgel."

"But 7B are having so much difficulty with that essay you suggested. You know the one: 'Who Am I?'"

"Pfft! 7B!" Vladimir snapped his fingers. "As I said, no brains."

"They have got brains, you know," said Ms. Dallimore, a little uncertainly. "One simply has to get them working. But oh, Vlad, that *awful* woman! She was so aggressive, and so *convincing*! She said I'd be reborn as a cockroach in the next life … I won't, will I, Vlad?"

"Of course not."

"Imagine being a cockroach!" Ms. Dallimore shuddered. "I couldn't bear it, Vlad! All that scuttling round in the dark, hiding from people—"

It didn't sound bad to Vladimir: he liked the dark, and he didn't have all that much time for people.

"What if she comes back?" fretted Ms. Dallimore. "That old woman? Sumati? When I fall asleep?"

"She won't." Vladimir gazed tenderly at her sweet white throat. "You work too hard, my lovely Madeleine, you wear yourself out with this 7B of yours. These brainless—"

"But Vlad! I told you they *do* have brains! They only need—"

"Hush!" Vladimir put a finger to her lips. "What you need, my love, is a vacation."

"A vacation! As *if*!"

"Far away in the mountains," Vladimir went on dreamily.

Ms. Dallimore clasped her hands. "Oh, that would be so wonderful!"

"In a castle."

"A castle? A castle, Vladimir?"

"A castle, my love," said Vladimir softly. "One day, not too far away."

How Many Words?

Once again Ms. Dallimore was struggling to stir a little creative enthusiasm in the citizens of 7B.

It was hard work, and beads of sweat glistened on her broad white forehead. "Paler," the Year Eight kids still whispered. "She's getting paler."

Ms. Dallimore surveyed her charges, those tender hearts and minds she had within her keeping. "Hearts and minds, my love?" Vladimir was always asking. "Are you sure they have them?"

"Yes, they do," Ms. Dallimore would answer, but as she looked around the room, something deep inside her faltered. Neema Grace had been staring out of the window for most of the period, Kate Sullivan was daydreaming. Molly Matthews was drawing a little border of tiny baby shoes around an empty page, Kerry Moss had her hand mirror out and was scowling at her chin. And as for Blocky Stevenson and his mates at the back, Tony Prospero and Leonardo Mack—

Ms Dallimore sighed. If only they would use their minds, if only they would think, imagine, fly! Why was it that anything that had to do with schoolwork seemed to turn their brains to stone?

Jessaline O'Harris raised her hand.

"Yes, Jessaline?"

"Ms. Dallimore, how long does this essay have to be?"

7B looked up from their various occupations because this was something they really wanted to know. How *loooong* did they have to write for?

"As long as you like," replied Ms. Dallimore.

"But, Ms. Dallimore, *how* long? How many words?"

"As many as you wish," said Ms. Dallimore, smiling. "Or as few."

"As few?"

"How few is few?" asked Leonardo Mack, and now every single soul was listening. For they did have souls, even though Vladimir kept suggesting that they mightn't.

"You mean, like—two hundred?" asked Jessaline.

"Or one hundred," said Tony Prospero. "Or, say, fifty?"

It was like some kind of dreadful auction.

"Fifty, Miss?"

"Could we do just fifty, Miss?"

Ms. Dallimore's head was whirling. "Less if you like," she said faintly.

Less?

How much less was less?

"Five words?" ventured Leonardo.

"One if you like," gasped Ms. Dallimore. "It could be one word—as long as you get the essence of who you are."

Essence? wondered Blocky Stevenson and several other people. Didn't that have to do with cakes? Cakes like Blocky's gran made: vanilla, that was one, and then there was lemon, and coconut …

"It's what makes a cake a cake, Brian love," Gran had told him, showing the tiny bottle with the red and yellow label. "It's an essence that goes all the way through, which makes the cake the sort of cake it is."

So with a person, Blocky figured slowly, essence would be what made you the sort of person you were. Which was? With him?

Well, footy for a start—no doubt about it, he was a footy person. But so were lots of other guys, and they weren't him. So what was the essence of him? What was Blocky essence? As he pondered, Blocky suddenly remembered that night when Ivy wouldn't lend him a pen, when she acted like he hadn't any feelings. And how he'd felt sort of all soft and hurt. Then there was how he felt with Gran: how he loved it when she showed him how to make cakes. It was as if, inside him, there was this person who— Blocky put a hand up to his head; his scalp had gone all tingly. What was happening? What was he doing?

He was—thinking. He was thinking about stuff, stuff that had to do with homework! How come? It had never happened before. It felt unnatural. Or did it? Blocky narrowed his eyes in Ms. Dallimore's direction. It was all her fault, she was to blame, she was *dangerous*!

One word! thought Kerry Moss scornfully. Like—like "bugger"! Or two words:"bugger homework"! That was her, all right, "bugger homework"! Imagine if she wrote that! Imagine Ms. Dallimore's face; the pale face that rose like a flower from her slender throat. There was a small red mark at the base of that throat which Kerry Moss knew was an ordinary love bite from that weirdo she went around with, even though the Year Eight kids said it was the mark of Dracula.

Dracula! Fat chance! scoffed Kerry. As if a *teacher* would be game for Dracula! And yeah, she just might write "Bugger homework!" for her essay. She was tough, wasn't she? She came from a tough family: Dad was a softie, of course, but Mum was tough, and Danny, and even little Charlie was showing signs of it: Miss Lilibet was talking about banning him from her nursery school.

Kerry was tough all the way through—except, if she was, then how come she couldn't stand some of that stuff on the TV news, stuff about wars and terrorists that worried her in bed at night so that she couldn't get to sleep and kept on whispering, "Please, God, please—"?

And how come she loved winter so much, especially those rare frosty mornings when the grass was all crinkly with ice and she'd walk across it because she loved the sharp little pinpricks of ice beneath her feet? "Kerry! Are you bloody crazy!" Mum would yell out through the fuggy kitchen window.

No, not crazy, thought Kerry. Not crazy, but real, sort of—*her*.

The bell rang.

Ms. Dallimore was glad of it: a single period always seemed like a double with 7B. She could feel a headache coming on; she'd be glad to get home and have a quiet dark evening with Vlad.

Blocky's head was feeling funny too. A few minutes back, when he'd been thinking, he was almost sure he heard a creaking noise inside it, like the sound of long unused machinery moving into gear. Blocky put his hand up to his head again; his elbow jabbed Tony Prospero in the chest. Tony punched Blocky on the arm, Blocky punched him back. Things were getting back to normal ...

7B erupted from the room, little bits of paper drifting from their pockets and their bags, the screwed-up abandoned beginnings of "Who Am I?" Ms. Dallimore followed wearily, turning left to the staff room and a reviving cup of tea. Halfway there, she felt an odd sensation in the middle of her back, a kind of burning. She turned and saw that frightening Mrs. Drayner glaring at her, her eyes like smoldering chunks of coal beneath her red plush hat.

Why? wondered Ms. Dallimore. Why would the chief school cleaner be glaring at her? Probably she wasn't, Ms. Dallimore decided. After all, Mrs. Drayner glared at everyone. "You have too much imagination, my love," Vladimir was always saying. Yes, that was it, thought Ms. Dallimore: she had too much imagination for her own good, while 7B had far too little for theirs.

Lucy Crying

Kate ran all the way home from school. She was glad it wasn't an afternoon for picking Lucy up from nursery school, because this morning ...

This morning she'd been woken early by the sound of a truck outside their house. When she looked through the window she saw big flat boxes propped against their garage wall. Kate knew what was inside them; she didn't need to read the labels that said "fragile" and "glass inside." The windows for her room had arrived!

"When?" she'd asked Dad.

"Watch my lips," he'd said, and Kate watched them pucker for the long *ooo* sound of his favorite answer: he was going to say "soon."

Only he didn't.

"Tonight," he said, and grinned at her. "Tricked you, eh? You thought I was going to say 'soon'!"

"*Tonight?*"

"That's right. I've got a day off and your uncle Jake's coming round to give me a hand." He snapped his fingers. "Nothing to it! We'll be finished by the time you get back from school. You'll be in there by tonight!"

And unbelievably, it *was* finished. She saw the glitter of those new windows the moment she flung open their back gate and ran into the yard. And she was, exactly as Dad had promised, "in there by tonight."

Kate looked around her new room. What did she love best here? Mum's curtains? "I made them ages back, love," she'd said. "But I thought I'd keep them secret till your dad got round to it."

Gran's brilliant tufty homemade rug in the middle of the floor?

The way her clothes and all her other things had their own private place, instead of being tangled up with Lucy's?

At the thought of Lucy, Kate's brows drew together in a small tight frown.

Lucy had been unusually quiet while the room on the verandah was made ready, and it wasn't till after dinner, when Kate's bed was moved in, that Lucy spoke at last. She came up to Kate in the hall outside their old room and stood right in front of her, so close that the toes of her running shoes touched Kate's. "Aren't you going to sleep in our room?"

"No, of course not," answered Kate. "I'll be sleeping in my new room. This is *your* room now."

Lucy's room had new curtains too, and another brilliant

rug from Gran—a woolly garden of birds and fruits and flowers.

"See?" Kate pointed at the small china plaque Mum had bought for Lucy's door. "See, it's got your name on it: 'Lucy.'"

"I know!" Lucy shouted. "I can read my name!"

"And that says 'room.'"

"I know that too!"

"Oh, well," Kate sighed, and then she'd run off because Mum was calling her. She hadn't seen Lucy since then, though she'd heard her yelling at Mum and Dad at bedtime, which was something she always did. But as Kate fell asleep, she kept seeing the way Lucy had stood in front of her out in the hall, with her back held very straight and her small fists clenched hard down by her sides.

Much later, Kate woke sharply; the glowing figures on her bedside clock showed half past two. The house was silent, yet a strange sound had woken her, Kate felt sure, and as she sat up and switched the light on, the strange sound came again.

"Aaarooo"—a low, painful keening, as if some small creature had been hurt out in the yard. Kate switched off the light again and looked out through the window.

Nothing moved: Mum's rose bushes stood black and straight beside the fence, the pegs on the empty clothesline perched like a row of frozen birds.

"Aaarooo!"

Kate turned. The awful sound was coming from behind the wall of their old room—from Lucy's room.

Lucy?

Lucy *crying*?

Lucy *never* cried.

She roared and shouted, hollered, yelled, protested, but she never, ever cried. Not when she fell off bikes and swings and monkey bars, not on her first day at nursery school, not even that time Charlie Moss had bashed her.

Could it be Lucy then?

That spooky noise?

Could it?

Kate crept out into the hall. The noise had stopped again; in the silence that followed, Kate heard a long, sobby sniff.

"Lucy?"

Lucy didn't answer. Kate opened the door and walked in. Light from the hallway showed that the bed was empty.

"Lucy?" There was a tiny movement from the floor. Kate looked down. Her sister lay curled on Gran's new rug, in the place where Kate's bed had been. "Lucy!"

Lucy shot up straight. "You're *mean*!"

"Mean?"

"You left me here!"

"But—" Kate knelt down beside her. "But this is your room now … Remember how you always kept on saying, 'This is *my* room'? Well"—Kate waved her hand—"now it is!"

Lucy sniffed. "But I thought it would still have you in it, when it was mine."

"Did you?" Kate put an arm round Lucy's shoulders. "Come on, Luce, you can't sleep on the floor, let's get you into bed …"

And somehow—Kate wasn't sure quite how it happened—there she was, on the first night of her new room, back in her old one, in Lucy's bed, with Lucy, hot and heavy, squeezed up by her side.

And there was worse.

"I want to go to the zoo," Lucy whispered damply against her sister's neck.

Kate said nothing.

"The *zoo*!"

"Yes, I heard."

"And Mum and Dad won't take me, they keep on saying 'soon.' And 'soon' is never."

"It mightn't be."

"Yes it *is*! And I really want to go; I've been wanting for years and years! Katie?"

Kate knew what was coming.

"Will *you* take me?"

Kate sighed. "All right, I'll take you one day."

Lucy's voice sharpened. "When?"

"Soo— I mean, um, I'm not sure just when."

"You were going to say 'soon'!"

"No, I wasn't."

"Yes, you were. Tomorrow? Will you take me tomorrow?"

"Not tomorrow; I haven't got time."

"Yes, you have. You've got the whole afternoon off school—Mum said."

Trust Mum. "I was going to ask Neema to come over and see my new room."

Lucy drew in a long, shuddering breath.

"Oh, all *right*," sighed Kate. She felt doomed.

White Sari

Neema and her dad sat on the garden swing, rocking gently, watching the last of the day.

"Did you see Nani's new running shoes?" asked Dad.

"Yeah."

"And the ones she bought for Sumati: purple, with orange laces? Your mum says she calls them flying shoes."

Neema nodded. She'd been wrong about Nani the other night: her great-grandmother wasn't thinking Neema's big white shoes were ugly; she was admiring them. The pair she bought for herself were exactly the same.

Perhaps she hadn't been thinking Neema's knees were knobbly, either, or that her great-granddaughter was the ugly person of the family. Neema had gone to her room that night and looked up "ugly" and "hideous" in the little English-Hindi primer Dad had given her; she'd been too embarrassed to go and ask her mum. None of the words she'd found looked like the one Nani had kept on saying: *nadi*. "Knees" was *ghutana* and Neema was almost certain Nani hadn't used that word. So she'd gotten all upset for nothing, and she might have upset Nani too, rushing from the kitchen as she'd done, in tears.

Above their swing the sky grew pale and tender, the clouds flushed pink, and for a moment the whole garden glowed; on the clothesline near the back fence Nani's white saris swayed and drifted, a row of airy ghosts pinned up on the wire.

"Dad?"

"Mmm?"

"Why does Nani always wear white saris and never colored ones?"

"Because she's a widow—white saris are widows' saris."

"But Gran wears colored saris, and she's a widow."

"Your gran's from a different generation; she's a modern city lady now."

"When did Nani's husband die?"

"Your great-grandfather? A very long time ago, in a cholera epidemic." Ignatius sighed. "He was only a boy, really—barely twenty. And your nani was only eighteen. Think of it, Neema! An eighteen-year-old girl left alone with a tiny baby daughter …"

That baby daughter would be bossy old headmistress Gran! It was hard to imagine Gran as a tiny fatherless child, but she had been all the same. It was easier to picture Nani as a sad young girl, already dressed in her white widow's sari, gently rocking a small child in her arms.

"Widow" sounded old, thought Neema, but Nani had only been a few years older than her, the same age as the Year Twelve girls at school. The Year Twelve girls in their vivid scarlet sweatshirts, who would leave next summer and begin their larger lives: going on to work and university, traveling, searching for adventure and fresh experiences, friendships and love, bright new worlds. Dressed in colors …

Imagine never wearing a color again: yellow, which made you feel happy, dashing red, peaceful blue, those flowery prints which told of summer coming, sunshine and long light days.

"You know," said her dad thoughtfully, "those little blue flashes on her new shoes must be the first color Nani's worn in nearly sixty years."

Sixty years! "What was he like, my great-grandfather?"

"No one really knows now, except for your nani and Sumati. Your gran was too young to remember him, and everyone else is gone. But I think he must have been a very special young man: certainly your nani loved him very much, and even Sumati liked him." Dad smiled. "That's the real test. Sumati's very hard to please."

"What was his name?"

"Raj."

From inside the house there came a sudden noisy clang and clatter. Neema and her dad exchanged glances. "Mum's tripped over the bucket again!"

"Sounds like it."

Nani washed her saris by hand, not in their rusty old

laundry tub, but in two big buckets she kept on the bathroom floor. Neema and her dad had learned to step round them, but Priya kept on tripping. The back door crashed open and she came limping toward them across the lawn. "Why can't she use the washing machine?" she exploded. "Why can't she? Or why can't she let *me* wash her saris? Why does she have to use those *buckets*?"

Going loopy, thought Neema, hearing the rising note in her mother's voice.

"Er—" began Dad.

"No, don't tell me." Priya raised a warning hand. "Don't tell me, because I *know!* She's an intelligent woman, she knows how to work the video! But she washes her clothes in buckets because Sumati does, because that's how Sumati's family did their washing a hundred years ago, up there in the hills."

Neema and her dad glanced uneasily toward the house.

"It's all right; she can't hear you, she's watching her film again! That song! It's driving me mad! It runs through my head all day! I hardly know who I am! Last night when I went into the study and switched my computer on to do some work—proper work, like I used to do—I started singing it. I started singing, *Beloved! After so long, to see your dear face once more*—"

Mum's eyes were round and shiny with bewilderment. She reminded Neema of Jessaline O'Harris: that time Jessaline had come up to her and Kate in the library and told them how she couldn't seem to get a start on Ms. Dallimore's essay.

There was an old school photo of Mum, Neema remembered suddenly—and in it, she had exactly those same tight, skinny braids as Jessaline. And now she made an abrupt little shaking motion with her head, as if, like Jessaline, she was twitching her own long-ago braids in dismay.

Priya gave a small choking sob and sank down onto the grass. "Sometimes I think"—she stared up at them with those big bewildered eyes—"sometimes I think I'll never hear Miss Dabke's mathematical music of the spheres again! Ever, ever again!"

Oh! Neema was horrified. Mum never to hear Miss Dabke's heavenly music—that was *bad*. Worse by far than mere bad temper or going a little loopy.

They sat down beside her on the grass. Ignatius put his arm around her shoulders; Neema patted her arm.

"Oh, don't!" She batted them away. "I'm being awful, I know. But I'm so sick of trailing round that Indian grocery, and watching that film, and cooking, and—and everything. Oh, I'm sorry, sorry."

Ignatius took her hand and tugged it gently. "Rise up, my darling; my fairest, come away. You need to delight in the garden, and to pick the lilies."

"What?"

"In plain old ordinary words, you need to take a little break, Pree. Tomorrow's Friday; why not go in to the university, to the Friday seminar?"

"The Friday seminar?" Priya's dark eyes glowed yearningly behind their tears. "Oh, if only I *could*!"

"Of course you can!"

"But how? I can't leave Nani all alone and go out by myself."

"I'll stay home," said Ignatius.

"But you can't; you've got patients tomorrow."

"I'll get a substitute," Ignatius said airily.

"Your patients *hate* strange doctors. Old Mrs. Pepperel slapped that last one's hand!"

"Old Mrs. Pepperel has since"—Neema's dad cleared his throat—"gone to live at Booligal with her long-suffering son." He slapped his knee and grinned. "And Booligal can have 'er!"

"Oh."

"So you can go tomorrow. To delight in the garden, and pick the lilies."

"But—"

Ignatius squeezed her hand. "Go, Priya, go!"

"Oh!" Tears welled freshly in Priya's eyes. Her mother had used those very same words when Priya had won her scholarship to Australia. *Go, Priya, go!*

"I'll ring that substitute," said Ignatius.

Neema took a long, deep breath. "No, Dad, you don't have to."

"Eh?"

"You don't have to miss work, Dad. I can stay home."

"But you've got school."

Neema took another long, deep breath: offering this meant she'd be alone in the house with Nani. For a whole long afternoon! But she offered anyway. "No, I haven't," she told them. "Not in the afternoon. It's a half day off, so—so I can keep Nani company."

They turned to her with hopeful faces, both of them. "Oh, Neema, would you?" begged her mum.

Neema nodded.

"Nirmolini," said her father. "Nirmolini, thank you. You are beyond price. Beyond all pearls and rubies. You are like—" He ran a hand through his thinning sandy hair and smiled at her. "You are like an apricot tree among the trees of the wood. Thank you."

Find Happiness: Retrain

Her English notebook open on the table, Big Molly Matthews was about to make a start on Ms. Dallimore's—or was it Count Dracula's?—essay. Tenderly she examined the subject of all her school compositions: her little blue baby shoes.

How perfect they were: how soft and sweet and—and small! Molly kicked off a slipper and measured a baby shoe against her large bare foot. The tiny slipper was scarcely larger than her big toe.

And then, out of nowhere, an awful thought seized Molly, squeezing at her heart, making her blood run cold. She was suddenly absolutely certain she had never worn those little shoes.

"Mum! Mum!"

Her mother's face appeared around the doorway. "Is something wrong, dear?"

Wrong? Molly's own moon-shaped face twisted horribly.

It was a thousand times worse than wrong.

"This!" She brandished the tiny blue shoes. "I never wore these, did I? Gran bought them for me, but I never wore them; I was too big the minute I was born!"

"Oh." Her mother at once guessed what was happening. "Hold on a sec," she said.

Hold on?

"I've got something I want to show you."

When Mrs. Matthews came back she had two old photographs in her hand. School photographs. "Look," she said to Molly. "That's me in Year Seven—the girl right at the back."

It could have been a photograph of the cast of Snow White and the Seven Dwarves, thought Molly: a giant person—Mum—rising from a crowd of little ones, like an enormous sunflower from a bed of daisies.

"But—?" began Molly, looking up at her mother with a puzzled frown. "You're not—"

"Exactly," said Mrs. Matthews briskly. "I'm no giant. And this"—she placed the second photograph in front of Molly—"is me in Year Twelve."

Now there were only daisies, tall and short and medium, but all daisies, no alien bloom in sight. "That's me," said Mrs. Matthews, pointing to a middle-sized girl in the center of the second row.

"Oh," said Molly.

"I was an early developer, like you are, Molly. A couple more years and those other"—Mrs. Matthews was a very tactful person: she didn't say "smaller"—"girls at school will have caught up with you, you'll see."

"So I *did* wear those baby shoes? They're really mine?"

"Of course you did. Of course they are. Look!" Mrs. Matthews turned one of the little shoes over; there were tiny scuff marks on the sole. "That's where you used to kick your little feet against the bottom of the pram."

Little feet. Molly's blood grew warm again; the squeezed-up feeling faded from her heart. "Oh," she breathed happily. "Oh." She could get on with her essay now.

She picked up her pen. And then she put it down again. She faltered. For years and years, since she'd become a big fat girl and thought she'd be one forever, Molly had believed that those baby shoes showed her real true self: the thin, delicate Molly buried deep inside her.

It had been about size, she realized suddenly; that was all. Now for the first time she thought, "There's more to me than size—much more."

"Oof!" Vladimir woke with a painful start. There was *light* in the room.

Beside him, propped against the pillows, Ms. Dallimore was reading.

"Madeleine! The light!"

"What? Oh, sorry, Vlad, I forgot." Ms. Dallimore flicked off the slim pencil flashlight she kept beneath the duvet.

"What were you reading, my love?" Vladimir twitched the skinny pamphlet from her fingers and scanned its shiny cover.

"It's wonderful how you do that, Vladimir," said Ms.

Dallimore admiringly. "Read in the dark, I mean."

"A humble talent, but all my own," said Vladimir modestly. "But what is this? This"—Vladimir read out the title—"*Find Happiness: Retrain!*"

"I was thinking of leaving teaching, Vladimir," said Ms. Dallimore sadly.

"Ah! Might one ask why?"

"It's so—*violent*. Oh, Vlad!" The teacher's voice grew tearful. "Mrs. Drayner attacked me today."

"Mrs. Drayner? This is the Indian lady in the colorful sari who stood next to our bed?"

"No, Vlad," said Ms. Dallimore, with the patience acquired from her dealings with 7B. "That old woman in the awful sari was a dream. Mrs. Drayner is real; she's the chief cleaner at our school."

"So? She attacked you, you say? For what?"

"It's the litter, Vladimir," replied Ms. Dallimore wearily. "The paper floating round the school. Some—well, quite a lot of it is bits of that essay you suggested I assign to 7B. Torn up, hardly begun—oh, Vladimir, those children simply haven't learned to *fly*!"

"Flying—ah!" sighed Vladimir.

"Perhaps I should have given them something simpler to start off, something like 'What I Did on My Vacation.'"

"Ah, vacation!" cried Vladimir, tossing the pamphlet aside. "Madeleine, do you long for peace?"

Ms. Dallimore thought of Mrs. Drayner's red plush hat and the faces of 7B. "Oh, yes!"

Vladimir looked pleased. "We will go on our vacation then, very soon."

"To the mountains? The castle?"

"Yes."

"Vladimir? What do you mean by 'castle,' exactly? What kind of castle? Is it one of those huge hotels?"

Vladimir didn't answer. His hooded eyes were closed.

Poor lamb, he's tired out, thought Ms. Dallimore.

My dear Sumati, wrote Kalpana.

At last I have bought our flying shoes. Air-pumped soles! Imagine, Sumati, air in shoes! That is what it says on the box, and that is what it feels like—not flying exactly, but as if you are walking on air. And in the shop I saw the skateboards again, Sumati. I took one down and held it, and turned the little wheels. So fast, so smooth—

Tick-tock, tick-tock, tick-tock—Kalpana rose from the chair and went to the window: every night at ten the flying boy came by. This evening she watched his feet carefully as he stopped beside the gate: how they moved and turned. And when they had waved to each other, she watched how he started again. Then she went back to her letter.

I held the skateboard in my hand, I was about to place it on the floor and try my foot on it—remember my dream, Sumati, about flying—flying so fast a little way above the ground that I would open a small crack in the world and see my Raj's face again? Well, on a skateboard one would be at exactly a hand's height from the ground. So I was about to place my foot on it, when along came Priya—you will guess the rest—all boss boss boss and rush rush rush. So I put the skateboard back upon the shelf, for now. But soon—some day soon, Sumati, I will learn to fly. And then, when I come home, I will show you, too.

PS I am glad you have made friends with Lakshmi's goat, and I understand how you would wish to bring such a good friend home. But remember the bus driver, Sumati! Remember the fate of the sweet potatoes!

.
.
.
.
.
•

Nani's Film

"Um, well, bye," said Priya, standing awkwardly in the doorway, all dressed up in her beautiful green suit and soft silk blouse. She didn't normally dress so grandly for a Friday seminar at the university, but today was a special occasion, the first time she'd been out on her own for weeks. She gave her daughter a swift, guilty kiss on the cheek. "I'll be back by five."

"Promise," demanded Neema.

"Promise."

"Cross your heart."

Priya's slender fingers sketched a quick gesture across the silky blouse. "Okay?"

"Okay," said Neema gloomily. It wasn't, though—Neema felt sure Mum would forget all about her and Nani the minute she reached the university.

Priya turned and hurried toward the grown-up safety of

her car. Her heart was thudding with a hard, swift beat, as it had on that afternoon many years ago when, after weeks of nagging, her mother had finally agreed to let Priya go roller-skating with her friends. She'd run down the street to the bus stop, afraid her mother would come hurrying after, calling, "Stop, Priya! Come back! I've changed my mind!"

Neema closed the front door. Now she was alone in the house with Nani. The door of the TV room was closed, but music swelled through it, billowing down the hall: Indian music that made your heart ache and then sent it soaring up again. Nani was watching her film. That was all right then, wasn't it? Nani didn't really need anyone to watch it with her; Neema didn't have to go in there …

"Why don't you ask Katie over?" Dad had said this morning as he left for his office. "Then there'll be two of you to keep Nani company."

But Neema hadn't seen Kate at school. They didn't share classes on Friday morning, and when Neema reached the school gate, late from her music period, Kate had already gone home.

Neema went to the phone and dialed Kate's number. "You only just caught me, love," said Mrs. Sullivan. "I'm off to work, I've got the afternoon shift today. And Kate's not here, either."

"She isn't?"

"No. And I'll tell you one thing, love, I'd much rather be going to work than where Kate's gone, any old day."

"Where's that?"

"She's taken Lucy to the zoo."

"*What?*"

"Yes! You could have knocked me down with a feather when she told me."

And knocked me down too, thought Neema, hanging up the phone. Kate taking Lucy to the zoo! Kate taking Lucy *anywhere*! Though Kate *had* been acting strangely lately: finishing Ms. Dallimore's essay before anyone else had begun …

The essay! Neema's was still upstairs, untouched. Having so much time to do it had simply made things worse: it gave you longer to worry and keep on putting it off. Or to make a start, as Jessaline O'Harris had, then crumple the messy pages up and leave them lying around.

"There has been a nasty increase in scattered paper," Mrs. Drayner had announced at the last assembly, "filthy pieces of"—she'd sniffed the word contemptuously—"*work*, barely begun, screwed up and chucked away."

Wentworth High must be the only school in the world where the chief school cleaner made announcements at assembly, reflected Neema, but the truth was that all the teachers, even the headmaster, were afraid of Mrs. Drayner. Neema had seen them stop mid-sentence when they saw her red plush hat bobbing past the windows of a classroom; they held their breath till she'd gone safely past.

Perhaps when the time came to hand the essay in, their English teacher might be gone, spirited away by Count Dracula in his big black car. But though Ms. Dallimore was growing paler every day, Neema simply didn't believe that story. Ms. Dallimore couldn't be the Bride of Dracula—she was a teacher, a sensible person, and she'd notice if her boyfriend acted strangely, wouldn't she?

No, Ms. Dallimore wouldn't vanish, so the essay simply had to be done. Neema glanced toward the door of the TV room; perhaps she could make a start on it now, and then she wouldn't have to watch that film with Nani. And if Nani came upstairs, she'd see at once that Neema was busy and— and she'd go away.

Make a start on *what*, though? Ten minutes later, Neema threw down her pen and pushed her workbook away. How could you say who you were when you kept changing all the time? She felt she was a different person from the one she'd been before Nani had arrived. She felt older, like the girl her real name, Nirmolini, had conjured in her mind. Only she wasn't kind and gracious as she'd imagined that girl to be. No, she was mean, she decided, thinking of Nani sitting alone in the TV room. Yes, *mean*.

Neema got up from her chair and went slowly down the stairs.

The film was like the music, thought Neema; first joyful, then sad, then soaring back to happiness again. And it was *hours* long: hours of meetings and partings, laughter, dancing and tears. Now, at last, they'd reached Nani's favorite scene, the one she liked to stop, rewind, and watch again. A young girl sat alone on a wide verandah, gazing sadly across a garden at a line of blue mountains, capped with snow. A young man appeared in the doorway behind her; she turned and saw him, the music swelled …

It was really soppy, but despite herself, Neema liked it too. She liked the way the boy looked at the girl, so tenderly and dreamily, as if she were the most perfect being who'd ever walked on earth. Would a boy ever gaze at her like that? Was it possible? A boy like—like Gull Oliver, she thought, and then, embarrassed with herself, pushed the thought away.

Nani pressed pause; the film froze on the young man's face. Neema quailed as Nani began to talk to her in Hindi.

"He is a little like my Raj," Kalpana told her great-grand-daughter. "In the way he looks at Rekha there, see? With that soft light in his eyes?"

The only word that Neema recognized was "Raj," which she knew now was her great-grandfather's name. Could it be that the boy in the film looked like him? Could that be what Nani wanted her to know?

Nani's Hindi flooded on, and Neema wanted to say something back, even if Nani couldn't understand her. "Um," she began awkwardly. "You—you can see he really loves her."

Nani's face lit up, almost as if she'd understood what Neema had said.

Perhaps she had. Dad said Nani probably knew some English, that she'd have picked it up when Gran was a little girl at school.

"Then why doesn't she ever *speak* any?" Neema had asked.

"Perhaps she's shy about it," Dad had said. "Perhaps she

thinks she'll sound funny—to us, I mean."

Nani wasn't shy in Hindi, though; her words flowed on, and Neema simply sat there, frozen, watching her great-grandmother's face, the big dark brilliant eyes that flashed and sparkled as she talked and then went soft and dreamy. And she found herself wishing something—not that Nani would go away, as she'd wished so many times, because it was all so embarrassing—but that she herself could understand her, even a little bit. She wanted to know what Nani was trying to tell her; she wanted to know about Nani, about her great-grandfather, and what it had been like growing up in India in the olden days.

"Of course his smile is not right," Kalpana was saying. "My Raj had a special smile for me, or for when he was very glad—a little groove, a hollow, would come into his face, just here." She touched a finger lightly to the side of her mouth. "I long to see that smile again, but you know, Nirmolini, I have never once dreamed of Raj. Sometimes I have this other dream, though: I dream I am flying, all by myself, a little way above the ground. Faster I go, faster and faster, and I know that if I fly fast enough, I will see his face again."

The credits began to roll; Nani stopped the film and pressed rewind. Now, thought Neema despairingly, she'll play it all over again.

And all at once she couldn't bear it: to sit for hours in this stuffy little room, where a thin strip of sunlight on the carpet was the only sign of the lovely afternoon outside. She grabbed hold of Nani's hand. "Nani, let's go out," she said impulsively. "Let's go out somewhere!"

·
·
·
·
·
•

At the Zoo

Taking Lucy to the zoo proved every bit as tiresome as Kate had expected it to be. No wonder Mum and Dad had chickened out.

The trouble began at the bus stop, where Lucy's sharp eyes fastened on the knees of a group of elderly ladies waiting for the number 43.

She darted forward; Kate grabbed her just in time. "Now listen, Luce," she said quite gently. "I don't want you to go saying things today. Things like 'It's snowing down south.' Okay?"

"I wasn't going to," replied Lucy virtuously.

Kate didn't trust her. When the 43 lumbered up the hill at last, she waited till the old ladies had settled themselves comfortably in the seats behind the driver's cabin, and then she led Lucy farther down the aisle.

"I want to be in the front!"

"Well, you can't. Just sit!"

Lucy sat. At the junction, an elegant lady boarded. She looked a little like Neema's mum, Kate thought, with her long glossy hair and beautiful shining eyes. She wore a dark blue dress, and blue stockings to match with a pattern of little clocks along their seams.

Lucy's eyes fixed on the stockings.

"Luce—"

Too late. Lucy pointed. "You've got legs like a Mullingar heifer!" she crowed, in a clear ringing voice that carried all around the bus. Heads turned, but Lucy's victim simply smiled.

"*Scusi?*"

"You've got legs like a Mullingar heifer!"

The elegant lady patted the front of her dark blue dress. "Speak no English. Only Italian, I—" and, pausing a moment to stroke Lucy's chocolate-colored hair ("Ah, *bella*!"), she walked on calmly down the aisle.

"Don't you ever say that to anyone again!" hissed Kate when they were safely out in the street.

"I didn't," said Lucy. "I didn't say 'snowing down south.'"

"I meant 'legs like a Mullingar heifer'!" Kate bawled out. Heads turned again; she thought she heard someone say, "Needs her mouth washing out with soap! And in front of her sweet little sister, too!" Kate lowered her burning face and walked on quickly, gripping tight to Lucy's hand.

"It's *rude*," she told her when they were out of range of the disapproving stares.

"Gran says it. Is Gran rude?"

She was, in a way, thought Kate. She'd been at their place on Sunday, rattling on to Mum about her neighbors, all of whom, according to Gran, were freaks and monsters, people whose petticoats always hung down south, above legs that should have belonged to Mullingar heifers … And Lucy had hovered in the kitchen, soaking up every word.

"It's different," she said to Lucy. "Gran's old."

"So when I'm old, I can be rude too?"

"Yes," said Kate shortly. "But not till you're a gran."

"I want to go back to the monkeys!"

"But we've *seen* the monkeys. We've seen them twice."

"Let's go and see them again."

"It's all the way over on the other side, Luce. Aren't you tired?"

"No."

Kate was tired. Her legs ached as she trudged back up the hill, her head felt dazed and swimmy, and there was a ringing in her ears from listening to Lucy's chatter. Why did her sister love monkeys so much? Was it because Lucy was *like* them? The smaller monkeys scurried and skittered like Lucy, they were never, for a moment, still; they jabbered incessantly, hooted with laughter, then turned cranky, roared …

"Look!" Lucy tugged excitedly at Kate's limp arm. "Look at that one, Katie! He's eating a banana! And"—she turned to Kate a face of sheer delight—"he *peeled* it, Katie! With his little spidery hands! He peeled it like a huming being!"

"Human being," Kate corrected wearily.

"Now he's throwing it away, and he's only eaten half of it, see?"

The banana had been lobbed outside the bars, almost at Lucy's feet. She bent toward it.

Kate grabbed her arm. "Don't touch it!"

"Why?"

"You'll get monkey's germs."

"Monkey's germs?" But then, the banana forgotten, Lucy shrieked out joyously, "Look! Look, Katie! Look at that big one over there! He's scratching his balls, like Grandpa does!"

"Lucy! What did I tell you when we got off the bus? What did I say about being rude?"

Before Lucy could answer, a sudden gust of wind whisked Kate's sun hat from her head and bowled it down the hill. It was her school sun hat, the one Mum said had cost a fortune; Mum would kill her if that hat got lost. "You stay there!" she ordered Lucy, and went pelting down the hill, snatching her hat up at the bottom, whirling around to check on Lucy. She saw with relief that her sister still stood where she'd been told, only now she had a small yellow object clutched tightly in her fist. She raised the object to her mouth and took a bite.

Kate's eyes bulged at the sight. The banana! Lucy had picked up the monkey's half-eaten banana! Kate raced back up the hill, so fast that trees and sky and people swirled around her like cake mix blended in a bowl.

"Lucy! Don't! Don't *swallow* it!"

Lucy gulped. "I *did*."

Panic surged in Kate. What happened if you ate a banana a monkey had been chewing? How sick did you get? Could you get rabies that way? Or something worse? Could you, even—*die*?

"Spit it out!"

"Can't!" Lucy opened a wet, empty mouth. "It's gone."

"Oh, Lucy!" Kate sank to her knees and pressed her sister close. "We've got to get you to the First Aid place."

Someone tapped her on the shoulder. "Look, we're sorry, but—"

Kate sprang to her feet. She saw Ivy Stevenson from Year Eight, and Kerry Moss's big brother, Danny.

"She swallowed the monkey's banana!" Kate wailed despairingly. "She's eaten a banana a monkey chewed!"

"No," said Danny calmly. "No."

"What?"

"She hasn't." Danny was holding a crumpled paper bag. "They were ours," he said, thrusting the open bag at Kate. Inside it were bananas.

"We gave her one of them," he said.

"It wasn't the monkey's banana your little sister was eating," explained Ivy. "It was a *huming* banana." Her full lips twitched to hide a smile. "Not fatal. If that's what you're so upset about."

"Are you all right?" asked Danny. "You look sort of red."

"*Very* red," said Ivy.

"I'm fine," said Kate stiffly.

"Oh, well. Sorry about that, then."

"Sorry about"—Ivy's lips twitched again—"the banana."

Oh, they were very sorry, thought Kate furiously. She could see their shoulders shaking with laughter as, hand in hand, they walked off into the scrubby bush-land behind the monkeys' enclosure. By nine o'clock on Monday morning the tale would be all around the school. A tear of rage slid down Kate's cheek.

"Katie? Katie?" A hand was patting her, patting her T-shirt, her arms, her damp hot sticky face. A small fat hand, with baby dimples still between its knuckles. "Don't cry, Katie. Don't be sad."

The unexpected tenderness that had overcome Kate last night swept over her again. It was no use pretending: Lucy had begun to change herself into a *huming being*. And Kate was changing, too: she was no longer a person who hated her sister—not always, anyway.

And that wonderful essay she'd written for Ms. Dallimore— those six whole pages of flying, perfect words about how she hated Lucy—was ruined. It simply wasn't true. It was gone. She'd never find anything to write in its place, never. She wouldn't be able to do it; she'd get into trouble.

Unless, thought Kate.

Unless Ms. Dallimore really *was* the Bride of Dracula.

·
·
·
·
·

Uran Khatola

Neema and Nani went to the park. It wasn't very far: along Lawrence Road and past the shops, around the corner and down the narrow lane behind the bowling green. Nani walked briskly, her small feet in their air-soled sneakers keeping pace with Neema.

"She's amazingly fit for her age," Neema's dad had remarked a few days after Nani had arrived. "Reminds me of Sister Josephine. Do you know, when Sister Josephine found me on their back doorstep, she would have been almost eighty, and yet—the way she *swooped* me up, out of the rain and that soggy old box, and *danced* me into the kitchen ..."

"Ignatius, you were only a couple of days old, you can't possibly remember that!" Neema's mum had protested.

"Indeed I do," Dad had said stoutly, with the same conviction that sounded in Molly Matthews' voice when she spoke of her mother fastening the buttons on her little baby shoes.

The park was deserted, long wavy shadows flickered from the trees, and the only sound was the crunch of their shoes on the gravel of the path.

Why was Nani so silent? wondered Neema as they walked on toward the lake. Why wasn't she talking on in Hindi, like she always did, like she'd been doing back in the TV room just a little while ago, talking and talking, even though Neema couldn't understand? She flicked a quick glance sideways—Nani's face looked stern, and even sad. Was she disappointed because she'd come all this way to find a great-granddaughter who didn't speak a word of Hindi? Who couldn't be bothered to learn? Neema felt her cheeks grow hot: she hadn't even opened that little English-Hindi primer except to find out if Nani had been talking about her big feet and knobbly knees. Nani hadn't seemed real to her, a person you might want to know.

Though Neema couldn't have guessed it, Kalpana's stern expression was only for herself. How foolish she was! How foolish she must have seemed to Nirmolini, back there in the house chattering on again, pouring out her thoughts and feelings in a language the poor child didn't know, on and on, like a river swollen in the monsoon rains.

"When you are old," she'd told her daughter Usha, "it's time to try new things. Time to be brave, to learn." And yet she didn't have the courage to speak those English words she knew. Kalpana pressed her lips together in a thin, straight line. The next word she spoke would be English. It would be. But what?

They sat down together on the grassy verge beside the lake. Neither of them spoke. Neema stole another glance at Nani. What was she thinking about as she watched the small waves washing in and out among the stones? Was she angry with her? But Nani looked sad rather than angry—perhaps she was thinking about her young husband, who'd died so long ago. Did she remember little things about him? Had she been trying to tell them to Neema when they were watching the film?

Neema looked out across the lake. Beneath the late summer sky, the water was a brilliant burning blue, the kind of blue you hardly ever see in real life, except in your pastel box, that favorite color you keep saving up for something really special. Yet it was the color of something she had seen once in the real world long ago, something splendid and perfect and … The color of the Indian sky, that was it! And with a rush it all came sweeping back: the warm, lovely evenings, sitting by the river with Nani and Sumati, squeezed safe between them, gazing up at a sky that was bigger than the one she knew back home, immense and blazing: Nani's sky. An important sky, so important, so vast and dazzling you'd think it would make you feel small. Only it hadn't. It had made Neema feel important and sure of herself, even though she'd been so little—as if who she was, and everything she thought and did, really mattered.

Lightly Neema touched Nani's arm. "Nani? Nani, I just remembered you, from when I was little, when we used to sit by the river, me and you and Sumati."

"Sumati," echoed Nani softly, and her face had the still, absorbed expression of a person making up her mind. "Yes!" she said, in English, so suddenly that Neema jumped a little. "Sumati, and me—and you. By the river. Us." She spoke slowly, haltingly, with a soft accent that Neema liked at once.

"By the river," Nani said again, more easily.

"What's 'river' in Hindi, Nani?"

"*Nadi*," replied Nani. "'River' is *nadi,* Nirmolini."

Nadi! It was the word Neema had imagined meant "gawky" or "ugly" or "knobbly-kneed." And all Nani had been asking was whether Neema remembered sitting by the river with her and Sumati!

Right! decided Neema. The minute she got home she'd find that English-Hindi primer, and she'd ask Mum and Nani about the words, and she wouldn't be shy about speaking them out loud, even if they did sound funny.

And then, abruptly in that quiet place, they heard a sudden swish and swirl of gravel from behind them, and a voice called, "Nirmolini!" It was a boy's voice, full of astonishment and a kind of joyfulness that made Neema think of the words her dad had said: "Nirmolini, your name like perfume poured out …"

She thought it sounded like Gull Oliver, but how could it be? She went quite still, holding her breath, afraid to turn around and see. Beside her, she heard Nani laugh and clap her hands. "*Uran khatola!*"

Uran khatola?

"Oh, Nirmolini! It's the—the flying boy!"

·
·
·
•
·
•

Nani Learns to Fly

Gull Oliver had been cruising down the path toward the lake, thinking, dreaming …

"I think best on the old skateboard," he told his mum on those evenings she caught him sneaking out when there was homework to be done.

"Now don't you go telling me it's schoolwork you're thinking about when you ride off on that thing! I wasn't born yesterday, you know!"

The funny thing was, it might be schoolwork. A problem that he felt stuck with, cooped up in his room, could somehow unravel as he sailed on through the quiet streets and the narrow, mysterious pathways in the park.

But these last few weeks it was Nirmolini he'd been thinking about. She obviously didn't remember how they'd met each other all those years ago. Once he thought she might: that time he'd seen her with Katie Sullivan, walking home from school. For a second, as she looked across the road, Nirmolini had seemed to recognize him, but then her eyes glanced away so quickly, bounced right off him, that he knew he'd only imagined it.

How could he get to know her again? You couldn't just walk up to a girl and say, "Hi, I'm Gull Oliver, remember me? I used to be your shepherd back at Short Street Primary. Seven years ago."

She mightn't even remember that there had *been* shepherds at Short Street Primary.

Skating by her house each evening he'd hoped to see her at a window so he could give her a little passing wave, and a smile—that would be a beginning, at least. But the only person he'd ever seen there was the old lady who waved and smiled at *him*.

How could he approach her? At school, she was always with other girls, a whole crowd of them, and that made it difficult to talk.

Gull sped up a little; he was nearing the end of the path now, the bit he loved best, where you came out from the shadow of the trees into the brilliant blue of lake and sky, where the light seemed to shower down. He soared out from the trees and—there they were! It was unbelievable, like a sort of miracle: beside the lake, the two of them, the old lady who always seemed to wear white, and—and *her*!

Her name flew from his lips. "Nirmolini!"

Kalpana left them together and stole quietly away; young

people needed to be on their own. She walked swiftly over the soft green grass, her small old limbs filled with the amazing lightness that comes from risking the thing you were long afraid to do. And it had been so easy, after all. She'd fretted and worried and been so proud, and then, when she'd spoken those first English words to Nirmolini, there hadn't been a trace of scorn or mockery on her great-granddaughter's face. Nirmolini had been surprised, that was all, and then she'd been—delighted.

Kalpana glanced up at the sky, where little pink clouds were sailing, and then across the water to the bank of silvery green trees on the other side. She knew this place, too, this park. Of course she did, and it seemed to her she had recognized it the very moment she spoke that first English word aloud to Nirmolini. She had looked up, and *seen*: seen how the water and the trees and the small scudding clouds were the ones of the place in her dream, the place where she would fly.

As she walked, Kalpana hugged Gull's skateboard to her chest, cradling it gently, as tenderly as Blocky Stevenson had cradled the old junior football he'd found in the cupboard beneath the sink. She was looking for a private little place, firm and flat and hidden, because when you were old and wanted to try something new, you needed to be private, away from the eyes of people who might fuss and bother, who might tell you, "Not that way, but this!" or even say, "You are too old; this you cannot do."

At last she found it: a small deserted parking lot, screened behind the trees.

Kalpana set the skateboard down. She placed one foot on it, then two. Exactly. Exactly so. There she was, a simple hand's height from the ground. She wobbled a little, and set one foot back firmly upon the ground. This would need practice; "Practice makes perfect!" Sumati was often saying. And practice took a little time. Kalpana glanced through the trees—over there, across the lake, Nirmolini and the flying boy sat talking. Hours might pass for them like seconds, she thought, smiling. She had plenty of time.

Her sharp old ears picked up two words from their conversation: "Count Dracula." Count Dracula? She knew what "count" meant, of course—that was numbers. But Dracula? What could that be? It wasn't a word she'd ever heard Usha say, and yet it seemed somehow familiar, as a word might be if you'd seen it on the cover of a book or on a big poster outside a cinema. "A fairy tale," she murmured. Dracula was someone from a fairy tale.

Gull and Neema talked for ages—shyly at first, then more confidently, and then as if they were very old friends and the seven years since they'd last talked together had simply melted away. They talked about many things, until, finally, their conversation came round to Ms. Dallimore. "Do you think her boyfriend really is Count Dracula?" asked Neema.

Gull shook his head. "It's just one of those teacher stories."

"You mean how people say Mr. Ruddy's on day release from a prison farm?"

Mr. Ruddy was the part-time woodwork teacher.

"Yeah. It's just because he's got tattoos and dirty finger-nails."

"So it's because Ms. Dallimore's so pale, and her boyfriend has that spooky car?"

Gull nodded. "But I reckon it's something else too. It's because she's the kind of teacher people remember, even when they're grown up."

"Like my mum remembers this little old lady who taught her math at university."

"And mine remembers the poetry teacher she had in Year Ten. Ms. Dallimore's one of them: a teacher you remember."

"Yes, she is," said Neema thoughtfully, and a vision of her English teacher floated into her mind: Ms. Dallimore as she might remember her when Neema was as old as Mum, or Gran, or even Nani; Ms. Dallimore in her long, swirly skirt, with her dark red hair and pale, pale skin, standing at the front of the classroom, talking about thinking, and imagination, and flying, and the heavenly music of the soul—

She glanced up suddenly. "Where's Nani?"

Neema and Gull stared round. The empty park stared back at them—the brooding lake, the hollow paths beneath the darkening trees.

"Could she have gone home?" asked Gull.

"No, no, she wouldn't," said Neema.

But where could she have gone?

And then they heard it, the faint tick-tocking sound of

little wheels, and far away on the other side of the lake they saw a graceful gliding figure, like a big white swan. Nani.

"She's—she's got your skateboard!"

Together, they began to run.

And now Kalpana was flying: the trees rushed by, and the water, and the small rosy clouds above, cool air brushed against her face, her sari floated out, all as it had been in her dream. Faster she flew, and faster—at any moment, as she pushed against the world, the tiny crack would open and she would see him.

"Nani!"

Faster. She needed to go faster now; only she couldn't, because Nirmolini was running toward her, and Kalpana could see how anxious her small face was, how her mouth shaped itself in a tight circle of alarm. "Nani, stop!"

"I need to go faster," Kalpana wanted to shout out loud, "I need to see! Oh, please!"

But there were tears sliding down Nirmolini's cheeks. "Aah!" sighed Kalpana, and she made the small graceful movements she had seen the flying boy make so many nights as she watched from the window of her room. And stopped.

Neema rushed up: she'd been so afraid Nani would fall, be hurt, but here she was, her feet quite safe and solid on the ground. "Oh, Nani!" Neema smiled as she took the old lady's hand. And this time it was her proper smile: the one that curved her soft lips upward and brought the tiny dimple, the small hollow, to show beside her mouth. The smile that made her face, for a precious instant, the perfect image of Kalpana's own lost Raj.

Dr. Vladimir Goole

"Come in for the seminar, love?" asked Veronica, the math department secretary.

"Er, yes." Priya found Veronica a little unsettling; she was so very forthright, and her voice was so very loud. And though Veronica was young and big and blond, there was something about her that kept reminding Priya of Sumati, Nani's old friend.

"Missed us, eh?"

Priya smiled. "Yes, I did. Do you know who's giving the seminar paper today?"

Veronica rolled her bright blue eyes. "Him."

Priya's heart sank. "Him," from Veronica, could only mean one person—Dr. Vladimir Goole.

"Dr. Goole?"

"Yup. Better you than me—he'll go on for hours in that drony old voice of his."

"It is a bit muffled."

"Keeps his lips half-closed, that's why," said Veronica. "It's to hide the fangs."

"Fangs?"

"Yeah. He's got these two really long sharp teeth at the sides." Veronica flicked a bright red fingernail at her own plush lips. "I saw them once when he snarled at me."

"He snarled at you?" gasped Priya, horrified. "What for?"

"For looking at the address on the back of one of those letters he gets from foreign parts."

"Where was it?" asked Priya curiously. "The address?"

"Trans—Transvaal? Trans something, anyway." Veronica took a roll of Koolmints from her desk drawer and peeled down the silver paper. "Have one?"

"Um, no thanks."

Veronica popped a mint into her mouth and spoke on through rolling peppermint. "The thing that gives me the creeps is those shades of his, the way he never takes them off." She chewed reflectively. "Makes you wonder what kind of eyes he's got behind them, doesn't it?"

"Dark ones, I suppose."

"You know what my Gustave says?"

Gustave was Veronica's six-year-old, who, with his little sister Theodora, was often to be found milling around the office after school.

"What?"

"He reckons there's no eyes there. He reckons it's just skin."

Priya shuddered. "That's horrible!"

"Yeah," said Veronica calmly. "Spooky. And Theodora, she reckons Dr. Goole's a vampire; she always wears her little silver cross around her neck when she comes in here after nursery school."

"Oh!"

Veronica shrugged her shapely shoulders. "Kids these days, eh? They get it all from videos." She leaned forward confidentially. "Have you ever met Dr. Goole's girlfriend?"

"I didn't know he had one."

"Oh, he has. Tall, red-haired girl, very pale. A bit dopey-looking—well, you'd have to be dopey to go out with him, wouldn't you?"

"I suppose so," said Priya uncomfortably.

"She's a teacher at Mum's school."

"Your mother's a teacher?" Priya was surprised. Veronica didn't seem the least bit like a teacher's child.

"Mum? God, no." Veronica chuckled amiably. "She's a cleaner—chief one, but. That's what my Harry calls her: Chiefie." Veronica chuckled again. "It really gets Mum riled."

He did look spooky, Priya thought ten minutes later, in the seminar room where Dr. Goole was holding forth. His hair was so very black, and his skin so very white—a thick sort of whiteness that made Priya think of a wreath of wax lilies in a funeral parlor. And those dark glasses were unnerving, especially after she'd heard what Veronica's little Gustave thought.

Priya shifted uneasily in her chair, and at once the dark glasses swerved toward her, balefully. She tried to sit still and pay attention, but a small face floated into her mind: Nani's face, with the absorbed and tender expression it wore when she made *ras malai*, or watched her crackly old film. When she caught sight of Neema walking into the room, or sat outside on the swing in the very early mornings, all by herself, gazing up at the sky. As if, thought Priya, Nani were listening to little Miss Dabke's heavenly mathematical music of the spheres.

Mathematical? *Nani*?

But perhaps there was other heavenly music, thought Priya suddenly, besides the mathematical. Music that Nani heard, and Neema, and Ignatius, and—and everyone. Perhaps—she stole a quick uneasy glance at him—even spooky Dr. Goole. What kind of heavenly music would he hear?

Somehow, it seemed better not to think of that. She thought instead of Ignatius's voice in the garden last night, Ignatius urging her to go in to the university, take a break, pick lilies—*Go, Priya, go!* And then her mum's voice, saying the exact same thing, all those years ago.

And Nani, too. Because now Priya remembered her mother telling her how Nani had said those very words to her when Mum was young and living in that dusty little town, where, miraculously, she'd won her scholarship to Delhi University. *Go, Usha, go!*

And if Nani hadn't fought for Mum to go to university, then she, Priya, might never have been able to go; she might have been stuck, her whole life long, in that little country town; she'd never have met Miss Dabke, perhaps never once heard the mathematical music of the spheres. She wouldn't have come here, either, so she wouldn't have met Ignatius, or had Neema for her daughter. Everything she had now had come from Nani.

"Oh, *Nani*!" Grabbing her handbag, Priya jumped up from her chair.

Dr. Goole's dark glasses swiveled angrily again. "Sorry," mumbled Priya, and bolted for the door. As it closed behind her, she thought she heard him snarl.

"Nice boy," said Nani as they hurried back home down Lawrence Road.

Neema said nothing.

Small fingers nudged her teasingly. "Nice boy."

"He's all right, I suppose," said Neema loftily.

They were late. Neema could tell by the light, and the way the shops were closed. If Mum was back, she'd be going loopy.

She *was* back. As they turned the corner, Neema saw the car parked outside the house, and Mum at the gate peering up and down the road.

Nani saw her too. She stopped. "Nirmolini?"

"Yeah?"

"Don't—don't tell." Nani made a small graceful motion with one hand.

"You mean the skateboard? Don't tell about the skateboard?"

Nani nodded, putting a finger to her lips.

"Our secret," said Neema.

It had better be. Mum would hate it. And as for Gran—if Gran found out, she'd be on the first plane from Delhi, she'd take Nani away from them at once, no chance to explain. And Neema didn't want Nani to go away.

Mum was running down the road toward them now, her makeup all smudged and her hair flying everywhere. Loopy, thought Neema, but not angry-loopy. Not yet, anyway.

"I thought you were lost!" Priya cried. "I've been looking everywhere! Oh, I'm so glad you're *home*!" Her brilliant smile was for them both, but it was Nani she rushed at, Nani she hugged tightly, in her trembling, open arms.

The Night Before

It was the night before Ms. Dallimore's essay had to be handed in, and 7B were struggling to get their thoughts a little above the ground. Some sat sternly at their desks or dining room tables, others slumped in armchairs or lay along the lengths of beds and sofas. They ate stuff to get them going: chocolate bars and bags of chips and peanuts and cookies and big bowls of ice cream in their favorite flavors. Jessaline O'Harris nibbled carrot sticks and slim green wands of celery. All of them wore strained and anxious expressions, as if they were trying to hear that heavenly music Ms. Dallimore had spoken of—the heavenly music of their souls.

When Neema asked her great-grandmother about "Who Am I?" she thought Nani might give her the kind of answer Dad gave: "You are my own dear Nirmolini, my precious jewel, my Rose of Shalimar …" Or some such.

But Nani didn't. Nani thought about it properly, as Ms. Dallimore said you should. And when she'd finished thinking, she made a small fluttery movement with her hand, and said, "This is very hard."

"I *know*."

"Like water, water sliding through your fingers; impossible to hold. Always changing, never still—"

Always changing, thought Neema. How *they* had changed, she and Nani, sitting companionably in Neema's room, talking happily to each other, when only a few short weeks ago there had been no words between them, and she had longed for Nani to go away.

Was there anything that didn't change? she wondered. That stayed there in the center of you, always the same? She thought of the way she'd felt when she was little, sitting by the river with Nani and Sumati: quite certain of herself and that she mattered, even under the important Indian sky. *That* was her.

It wasn't an idea you could easily put into words, and Neema didn't even try. Instead she took the deep blue pastel from her box, the special one she hardly ever used, and colored in a whole sheet of paper. "This is the Indian sky," she told Nani. "See?" Then she wrote her name, her real name, Nirmolini, in graceful looped letters right across the sky. "And this is me."

Blocky Stevenson had found a pen—and football cards, and glue. Carefully he pasted the cards in three neat rows across the page: they looked really great, and they covered three-quarters of the sheet.

"I am a person who likes Aussie Rules football," he printed underneath them, and then, in bigger letters, "BUT I AM NOT A LEATHERBRAIN."

There wasn't much room left now, only a small narrow strip at the very bottom of the page. Blocky was rather glad about that, because the last sentence was so embarrassing he was relieved he had to write it small: "*I am a person with feelings.*"

"I was a brainy girl," wrote Jessaline O'Harris. "Or at least I thought I was. Until I began this essay, until I—" Jessaline stopped and stared down at the page. What was she *doing*? She was writing an essay about writing an essay. You couldn't do that, could you? That wasn't "Who Am I?"

"Heavenly music," she thought suddenly, remembering Ms. Dallimore's strange words. "The heavenly music of my soul," pondered Jessaline. What would that sound like? Like the rattle and roll of used-up pens tossed upon the floor, the scrunch and rip of paper … Jessaline sighed, and scrunched and ripped.

In the room next to hers, through a very thin wall, Jessaline's parents tried not to listen to these sounds. They sat side by side, propped against their pillows, spectacles on their noses, reading. Mr. O'Harris's book was called *Problems in Adolescence*. Mrs. O'Harris's was called *Feel Good About Your Awful Child*.

—

"I am a Big girl," wrote Molly Matthews. "And only a little while ago I thought that was truly me, *all* of me, forever—just Bigness, BIG BIG BIG. But now—"

Molly gripped her pen firmly, and filled her strong young lungs with air. She cast a quick fond glance toward the shelf where her baby shoes now lay, next to her favorite old teddy bear. "You're lovely," she told them, "but now—I'm leaving you behind."

"Once I was a person who hated my little sister," wrote Kate. "That was me. But now I don't hate her anymore, not really. I changed, so—"

Kate stopped and began chewing fiercely at her bottom lip. What came next? What could she write? What?

"So—so now, I don't know who I am," she scribbled quickly, and tossed her pen aside. She wasn't doing any more; she *wasn't,* that was that. After all, hadn't Ms. Dallimore said it didn't matter how long or short their essays turned out to be?

"She didn't mean it, I bet," muttered Kate furiously.

There was only one hope: Kate closed her eyes and crossed her fingers upside down. "Please," she whispered fervently, "please, Count Dracula, *tonight*—take Ms. Dallimore away!"

A Shock for Mrs. Drayner

Mrs. Drayner had been visiting her daughter Veronica, and Veronica's children, Gustave and Theodora. "The other party," as Mrs. Drayner was in the habit of calling her son-in-law, had been absent from the home. Makes himself scarce when I come round, thought Mrs. Drayner with satisfaction.

On the way home she got off the bus at the stop for Wentworth High.

She often did this: she liked to cruise the school at night, checking the mayhem wrought since she'd left the place—spotless—at exactly half-past two. The classrooms and corridors were a little scuffed, but you had to allow for that—kiddies were kiddies, after all. The staff room was another matter: a rats' nest, a littered, filthy *hole*! "Raised in creekbeds, the lot of them," grumbled Mrs. Drayner as she slammed the door.

Down the covered walkway she went then, her heels tiptupping briskly, her red plush hat bobbing bravely on her head. She entered the library, where, last period on Mondays, 7B had something called "free study."

The floor was covered with snow. That was what Mrs. Drayner thought when she first switched on the light. Then she saw it was more of those bits of paper this class kept throwing away. She picked up the one that had nestled against her foot the minute she opened the door. *Kerry Moss*, it said at the top, *Class 7B, Who Am I?*

People think I'm tough, read Mrs. Drayner, in Kerry's generous scrawly hand. *Just because my mum is! Because Mum scared a teacher so much he ran away from school.* "Good on 'er!" muttered Mrs. Drayner. "One less of 'em to pick up after!" *But they're wrong*, continued Kerry. *I am—*

And there it stopped, as they all did. Beneath the red plush hat, Mrs. Drayner's mouth set grimly: she knew who was responsible for this. She'd have another go at that soppy Ms. Dillymore tomorrow. "Who Am I?" indeed!

But who am *I?* she asked herself suddenly. She knew who people *thought* she was: a ragged old soul, born to sweep and scour—and lonely sometimes, since her lovely Neville had passed away. But that wasn't all of her, not by any means! Mrs. Drayner raised a hand and stroked the soft plush of the hat she'd found in the window of St. Vinnie's. It was the same one, no matter that Veronica said it couldn't be—the very same hat Mrs. Drayner had worn in her Grade Six year, in the school production of *Cinderella*.

Oh, how she'd cried when she'd had to give that hat

back to the school! Yet see how it had come back to her, by some magic roundabout of circumstances. "Life's a dizzy old whirl sometimes," murmured Mrs. Drayner. She hadn't been Cinderella in that play, or one of the ugly sisters; she'd been the Prince's page. She'd worn a beautiful little green suit her mum had made for her, white shoes and stockings, and the wonderful red velvet hat. She'd carried a bell: "Oyez! Oyez!" she'd sung. "Come, maidens, come! Try on our royal shoe!"

And she'd stolen the show from all of them: five curtain calls she'd had to take. She'd walked home with her proud parents, feeling light as air.

And wasn't she still that same person, deep down inside? Of course she was! No doubt about it! Mrs. Drayner's chest swelled proudly. "Oyez! Oyez!" she sang, in a voice of such astounding beauty that poets might have sung of it, and probably had, in those slim neglected volumes in the farthest corner of the library.

But—what was that roaring noise outside? Mrs. Drayner hurried to the window and peered out into the night. On the road outside, in a blaze of streetlight, she saw a big black car. "Like a hearse," she told her family later, "like something Count Dracula would drive." As she watched, the tinted passenger window slid down and she thought she glimpsed a pale familiar face—that Ms. Dillymore! "Gadding round in hearses now!" exclaimed Mrs. Drayner angrily. "Whatever next? These teachers!"

"Whatever next" made the tiny hairs stand stiff along Mrs. Drayner's spine. For with a final, deafening roar, the big black car rose up steeply from the ground!

"Went right up, it did," quavered Mrs. Drayner later in Veronica's comfy living room, wrapped in a blanket for shock and sipping hot sweet tea. "*Right* up, before my very eyes. And, and then …"

It flew away. In a northerly direction, up through the clouds, between the moon and stars, heading for a castle in the mountains, in a far-off foreign land.